Praise for Lexi Blake and Masters and Mercenaries...

"I can always trust Lexi Blake's Dominants to leave me breathless... and in love. If you want sensual, exciting BDSM wrapped in an awe-some love story, then look for a Lexi Blake book."
~ *New York Times* bestselling author Cherise Sinclair

"A master at sexy, thrilling romance."
~ *New York Times* bestselling author Jennifer Probst

"Lexi Blake can do no wrong!"
~ *New York Times* bestselling author Carly Phillips

"Lexi Blake has set up show on the intersection of suspenseful and sexy, and I never want to leave."
~ *New York Times* bestselling author Laurelin Paige

"Smart, savvy, clever, and always entertaining."
~ *New York Times* bestselling author Steve Berry

"Lexi Blake's MASTERS AND MERCENARIES series is beautifully written and deliciously hot. She's got a real way with both action and sex. I also love the way Blake writes her gorgeous Dom heroes-- they make me want to do bad, bad things. Her heroines are intelligent and gutsy ladies whose taste for submission definitely does not make them dish rags. Can't wait for the next book!"
~ *New York Times* bestselling author Angela Knight

"Ms. Blake's writing draws you in and will keep you riveted from the first chapter to the last."
~ Erin, Thelma and Louise Book Blog

"I can't get enough of the Masters and Mercenaries Series! Love and Let Die is Lexi Blake at her best! She writes erotic romantic suspense like no other, and I am always extremely excited when she has something new for us! Intense, heart pounding, and erotically fulfilling, I could not put this book down."

~ Shayna Renee, Shayna Renee's Spicy Reads

Devoted

Also by Lexi Blake

CONTEMPORARY ROMANCE

Taggart Family Values
Treasured
Delighted
Tempted

Masters and Mercenaries: The Forgotten
Lost Hearts (Memento Mori)
Lost and Found
Lost in You
Long Lost
No Love Lost

Masters and Mercenaries: Reloaded
Submission Impossible
The Dom Identity
The Man from Sanctum
No Time to Lie
The Dom Who Came in from the Cold

Masters and Mercenaries: New Recruits
Love the Way You Spy
Live, Love, Spy
Sweet Little Spies
The Bodyguard and the Bombshell
No More Spies
Spy With Me
Love and Let Spy, Coming March 24, 2026

Butterfly Bayou
Butterfly Bayou
Bayou Baby
Bayou Dreaming
Bayou Beauty
Bayou Sweetheart
Bayou Beloved

Park Avenue Promise
Start Us Up

My Royal Showmance
Built to Last

Lawless
Ruthless
Satisfaction
Revenge

Courting Justice
Order of Protection
Evidence of Desire

Masters Of Ménage (by Shayla Black and Lexi Blake)
Their Virgin Captive
Their Virgin's Secret
Their Virgin Concubine
Their Virgin Princess
Their Virgin Hostage
Their Virgin Secretary
Their Virgin Mistress

The Perfect Gentlemen (by Shayla Black and Lexi Blake)
Scandal Never Sleeps
Seduction in Session
Big Easy Temptation
Smoke and Sin
At the Pleasure of the President

Texas Sirens
Small Town Siren
Siren in the City
Siren Enslaved
Siren Beloved
Siren in Waiting
Siren in Bloom
Siren Unleashed
Siren Reborn
The Accidental Siren

The Reluctant Siren

Nights in Bliss, Colorado
Three to Ride
Two to Love
One to Keep
Lost in Bliss
Found in Bliss
Pure Bliss
Chasing Bliss
Once Upon a Time in Bliss
Back in Bliss
Sirens in Bliss
Happily Ever After in Bliss
Far from Bliss
Unexpected Bliss
Wild Bliss
Brooke's Bliss

Standalone
Away From Me
Snowed In

ROMANTASY

Thieves
Steal the Light
Steal the Day
Steal the Moon
Steal the Sun
Steal the Night
Ripper
Addict
Sleeper
Outcast
Stealing Summer
The Rebel Queen

Devoted

Masters and Mercenaries:
Sanctum Nights
Book 6

Lexi Blake

Devoted: Masters and Mercenaries: Sanctum Nights, Book 6
Lexi Blake

Published by DLZ Entertainment LLC

Copyright 2014 DLZ Entertainment LLC
Edited by Chloe Vale
Print ISBN: 978-1-963890-48-8

McKay-Taggart logo design by Charity Hendry
Masters and Mercenaries ® is registered in the U.S. Patent and Trademark Office.
Lexi Blake® is registered in the U.S. Patent and Trademark Office.

Sign up for Lexi Blake's newsletter
and be entered to win a $25 gift certificate
to the bookseller of your choice.

Join us for news, fun, and exclusive content
including free short stories.

There's a new contest every month!

Go to www.lexiblake.net to subscribe.

Acknowledgements

Thanks as always to Liz Berry, MJ Rose, and the entire crew at 1001 Dark Nights. Thanks to the amazing editors, Kim Guidroz and Pam Jamison and my betas, Stormy Pate and Riane Holt. Thanks to my husband and kids for always being there.

This book is dedicated to several amazing men who helped shape my life and who taught me to see the world through different eyes. To Chad from Bell High School. To Lyle from my college years at UNT. To Lee, who is always there for me. And to Christopher, the latest in a long line of men I adore and who prove that you can find love and understanding without ever having sex.

But don't worry, there's totally sex in this book....

Chapter One

Amy Slaten hung up the phone and sighed.

"Not again."

She kind of wished her ex-husband wasn't here to witness her complete and utter humiliation. Unfortunately, her ex-husband also happened to be her best friend and had been her business partner for a very long time. Their firms had been kept separate by an ironclad prenup and they'd handed back each other's stock after their amicable divorce, but still she turned to him in times of trouble.

And the times they were a troubled now.

"Yes, we lost the Kleinman account. They're concerned about the lawsuit and how my father could keep us wrapped up in court for a long time. Naturally they went to Glendale." Glendale Incorporated was the bane of her existence and had been for a long time. She'd heard the company was under new management since John Adler had died. John and her father had been business rivals, and not the friendly kind. They'd gone for each other's throats and it looked like the son John, Jr. was planning on keeping up the family traditions. He came after every contract Slaten Industries had, competed for every one they went after. Even the ones they shouldn't. Glendale was so much bigger than Slaten. They shouldn't play in the same sandbox, but the Adlers seemed determined to wipe out Slaten no matter what the cost to their own company.

Frankie sat back, his perfectly tailored clothes not wrinkling at all. He was wearing a Dolce & Gabbana three-piece suit with a snowy white dress shirt and a peacock blue tie that nearly matched his eyes. He was the most stunning man she'd ever met.

Unfortunately, he was also gay. Their marriage, while loving and friendly, had not been intimate in a physical sense.

"Is there anything I can do?" Frankie asked. "Beyond assassinating your father? Because I could arrange that. I know some interesting people."

She had to chuckle at that. "Don't tell me you're bringing in the gay mafia."

His lips curled up in a perfectly gorgeous smile. "Don't underestimate the gay mafia, darling. They will take care of business and with amazing style." He sobered. "You know I would do anything for you, right?"

He'd proven that when he'd married her in order to help her take Slaten Industries away from her awful father. At the time her father had been planning to sell the company her grandfather had built and take all the profits for himself. He'd been willing to sell out every employee they had for his own gain.

She'd stopped that with Frankie's help, and she'd used the stock she'd gotten on the day she'd married him to help him wrest power away from Hank Lyndon, Frankie's father and chief tormentor. They'd bonded over horrible parents.

His company was running brilliantly. Hers not so much. She was dealing with a board filled with relatives waiting to stab her in the back, chaos from moving the main office to Dallas along with her entire staff, multitudinous lawsuits filed by her parents, and a never-ending blood feud she didn't quite understand.

All in all, her stress levels were reaching maximum capacity and she wasn't sure she could come back down.

She bit back tears as she looked at him. There was no crying in CEO land. "I do and I thank you for it, babe, but unless you know John Adler, Jr. and can force your will on him, I think I'm screwed."

"Let me look into it. Will you at least let me look into him?"

She winced. It wasn't the first time he'd offered. The trouble was she didn't want to play the way her dad did. Her father had kept dirt on every single business rival he'd had. He'd had files on all his perceived enemies. When she'd taken over the company, she'd inherited all of them and promptly burned them.

Her father kept files on everyone, including her and her sister, Bridget. She could still remember looking through her own file.

Amy is weak. All it would take to deal with her would be to send in a man who could make her feel pretty. With the right man in place, she will be completely controllable.

Lucky for her the "right man" in her father's words had been the one who could make him money. He'd made a deal with Frankie's father that would benefit the both of them, and neither gave a damn that their kids had plans of their own. It had worked out for her and Frankie in the end.

But she'd learned to never trust a man like her father.

Frankie was different, but he could be just as ruthless when it came to someone he loved. She was determined to never behave like that. If she won, she would do it fairly.

"I don't want to come at him personally," she said. "He's done nothing like that to me."

"You don't think he's playing dirty?"

"I don't think he's coming after me on a personal level," she clarified. "This is business, babe. You know as well as I do that it can be cutthroat and nasty and not personal."

"So if you met this asshole, you wouldn't slap him?"

She had to laugh at that. "I would buy him a drink and ask him what the hell my father had done to his. Seriously, I would do that in a heartbeat. And I would flirt shamelessly with him."

Of course, he was very likely thirty years older than she was and probably married with kids or even grandkids. His father had been eighty when he died. If he'd been like her parents, he'd had kids in his twenties and that would make them in their fifties or sixties, so her flirtation likely would be for naught.

Frankie grinned. "And he would fall madly in love with you and all of this would be over."

He could also be an optimist at times. "I doubt that, but I would ask. Unfortunately, I'm not likely to sit across a table from him. He

19

won't meet with me and I'm not flying back to California to force a meeting. We've got another shot in a month. If we can get the Clannahan account, we'll be in the black for another six months. And I can flirt with those men."

They were an Irish company looking for an American company to make a deal with. They had all the access to European markets that Slaten needed to grow. In exchange, Slaten could give them a position in the States. It would be a win-win for both companies.

If she could only convince them. Everything was on the line. Everything she'd worked for. All the jobs she'd tried to save. They would be gone if she didn't manage to make this work.

"You know I want to help you in any way I can. I love you, honey," Frankie said quietly.

Tears misted her eyes. After her sister had left home, she'd thought she would never find another person she could count on, but she'd met Frankie in college. She'd had boyfriends and lovers and a couple of wild nights she didn't wholly remember, but she'd only loved one man. Unfortunately, he was attracted to men. She'd accepted that a long time ago.

"I love you, too, but you can't force my father to drop the lawsuit. We sincerely pissed him off and he won't give up easily."

"How about the other issue?" Frankie asked, his eyes trained on her as though attempting to detect any untruth she might give him.

He had good reason for that. She'd been trying not to worry him. It was her problem after all, and she was a big girl. "Are you talking about Ray Paulsen? I've got lawyers working on that, too."

Frankie leaned forward. "He's unstable, Amy."

"Which is one of the reasons I had him fired." Ray had been her father's head of security. Amy had considered him little more than the asshole who intimidated everyone so that her father got his way. She'd been more than happy to show him the door the minute she'd taken over the company.

"He swore he'd get you back for that," Frankie pointed out.

"And he's suing me, too," she said. She was so tired of lawsuits.

Frankie didn't seem convinced. "I'm going to look into that asshole. He's not the type of man who would be content with simply suing you. I want you to be careful. The minute anything feels wrong, you call me."

And have a bodyguard put on her ass? "I promise. But he's not an idiot. He knows if he harasses me and I catch him it won't help his case. Besides, the last time I checked, he was still in California, half a continent away. Aside from Ray and my father, the good news is we're truly the best fit for Clannahan. I think after we meet next month they'll understand it, too. Then I'll be in a better position to deal with all of dear old Dad's crap."

She was going to be positive. Change wasn't easy. It was difficult but everything that was meaningful in life was hard to achieve. She'd managed to break away from her father. She'd moved her company and her life across the country to be closer to her sister. She'd made deals with the city that ensured she could bring her people with her. Tax incentives had given her the cash to offer any employee who wanted to move the wherewithal to do it. Slaten would be stronger here in Dallas. She'd lowered their costs across the board for years to come with this move and she'd offered good compensation to the few employees who'd chosen to stay behind. They would build a company that served its employees and not the other way around.

She was strong. She could do this.

Frankie reached across her desk to put a hand over hers. "I know they will. Are you really going through with tonight?"

The question made her grin because she was totally going through with tonight. "Does the thought scare you?"

He frowned. "The thought makes me kind of want to go and get my own membership at Sanctum so I can be your training Dom."

That was absolutely the last thing she wanted. For the last couple of years she'd used Frankie as a protective wall, a reason to not put herself out there. She was done with that. She loved him so much, but she needed more. First and foremost, she wanted a damn orgasm that wasn't battery operated. "You would never be assigned to me because they pay attention to what a sub needs. I had to fill out a freaking book on what I need. Do you know one of the things I need? A penis that might want to slip inside me and rub one out."

His eyes closed, a grimace coming over his perfect face. "Do you have to be so forthright?"

She kind of loved it when he got all prudish. He was not a man

21

who ever should take that attitude since she knew damn well he'd had some wild nights himself. "Mama is stressed. Mama needs a little something something, if you know what I mean."

He put a hand out. "I do. Please don't tell me about it in detail."

Where was the fun in that? "I'm not planning on jumping the poor man or anything, but if it comes up, I'm ready and willing to get three kinds of kinky."

It had been a rough eighteen months. Between the takeover and her pre-planned divorce, it had been hard. There hadn't been a ton of time for dating. She'd focused entirely on Slaten Industries, and she was ready to have a few hours a week to relax and work on herself. And to be around a man who might want to put his penis inside her.

That was a definite goal.

Frankie stared at her for a moment. "Sweetheart, how much have you dated since we got married?"

She smiled on the outside. Inside she was punching something. This was a conversation she'd been trying to avoid. "I've been busy."

Frankie leaned in. "When was the last time you had sex?"

She felt herself flush. "Before we got married."

She wasn't a prude. Far from it. She liked sex, but she took the marriage thing seriously. Even when he hadn't. Frankie had spent their wedding night with his boy toy of the moment.

No honeymoon for Amy.

So she should have a post-divorce bacchanal complete with tons of wine and a super hot Dom. Not necessarily at the same time.

"I thought we talked about that." Frankie had his concerned face on.

Yep, this was why she wanted to avoid this conversation. "We did. I made a decision to honor my vows. You know what my parents are like."

His father screwed anyone with a skirt—and that did not necessarily mean a vagina—and her mother regularly made love to her bottle of Chardonnay and the pool boy. She'd grown up with constant cheating. She couldn't stand it. Her marriage might have been a sham, but she respected it.

"I do, sweetheart. I'm so sorry. I should have been better."

One of the reasons she'd avoided this talk was because the last thing she wanted was to make him feel guilty. "I made that choice, Frankie, and it had next to nothing to do with you. It was something I needed to do. Now that I'm single I intend to be as skanky as possible. I'm serious. I want to tear through some dicks."

Frankie turned a nice shade of pale. "Again, not something I needed to hear from you."

"So you want me to take notes? We could have a sleepover and talk about our sex lives."

He stood and straightened his suit. "I shudder at the thought. I have to be at the airport in an hour. Unless you change your mind. I could talk to Taggart and have a membership very quickly. I wouldn't have to be your training Dom. I would merely ensure that the one selected for you understands how he should treat you."

She shook her head as she rose to hug him. Nope. She didn't need her ex-husband giving her potential fuck buddy a lecture. No how. No way. She was letting her hair down and forgetting about work and having fun for once in her life. "There's a very careful vetting process to ensure we're compatible and not psychotic. I'm fine. Now go. Have fun in San Francisco."

He held her close. "I'll call. Be careful, Amy. I know you want to have fun, but be careful around those men. They can be rough but you need to remember that you're the one in control. And listen to your sister. She knows this world better than you do."

Her sister wrote about the world of D/s. Bridget was a romance author and had quite a career. Of course, she also wrote what she liked to call mega ménages, where one woman ended up with five or six men all desperate to service her. Bridget lived in a fantasy world and didn't pay a lot of attention to the one outside of it. She was also super pregnant with her first kid and not playing a ton these days. Still, if it made Frankie happy to think Bridget was watching over her, she would go with it.

She kissed his cheek and watched him walk away. The man was fine either way he went. Coming or going.

"Ms. Slaten, you have a call on line two," her assistant said, poking her head in the door.

Amy sighed. "Thank you, Val."

Tonight she wouldn't be Ms. Slaten. She would be Amy or pet or whatever her training Dom wanted to call her.

Only hours to go before she could spend some time in another world. Hopefully it would be better than this one.

* * * *

John Flynn Adler, Jr. stared at his brother from across the bar that separated Mitch's kitchen from his living room. Perhaps he hadn't understood. Maybe having a child had turned Mitchell's brain soft. "What do you mean?"

Mitchell Bradford was his half brother. For much of his life, Mitch had been a complete mystery to Flynn. It had only been when their father was dying that he'd connected with his brother. Getting close to Mitch and his wife, Laurel, had been exactly what Flynn had needed at the time.

At the time? He needed it now. He might always need it. Mitch was a taciturn son of a bitch, but he was a great brother. Chase, their youngest brother, was now in college and doing better than Flynn would have imagined and it was all because Mitch had stepped up. Chase lived in Mitch's guesthouse and was treated like a member of the family by Laurel, who ensured the kid ate something other than mac and cheese.

Sometimes Flynn envied his kid brother. His Victory Park condo had amazing views and he'd discovered it meant nothing if he had no one to share it with.

"Amy Slaten is the partner Kai and Wade selected for you to work with. I peeked at the list when I was reviewing some of Sanctum's business contracts." Mitch patted his son on his back in a rhythm only he could hear. He carried Johnny around a lot as the boy seemed determined to only sleep on top of other human beings. "I swear if I'd known she was going to be in that class, I would have moved you to another one. I only figured it out this morning. In their defense, they don't know about the corporate war the two of you are involved in. Both companies have been very careful about keeping it out of the press. So should I talk to Wade or do you want to do it?"

Amy Slaten. His nemesis, according to the man who ran his company. Amy Slaten was following in her father's very ruthless footsteps by sending spies into his company and hacking in to steal their data.

Oh, she looked all soft and sweet. She was a gorgeous woman. He'd seen her at a few functions but had chosen not to be introduced. Since he'd handed over the reins of the company to a hired CEO and changed his personal focus to R&D and raising Chase, he tried to stay out of that particular war.

He was still listed as the president of the company, still the figurehead, but he preferred to work on the creative side. When he'd left California behind, he'd tried to start over. The new software he was developing would change the way his clients did business.

The last thing he needed was to get involved in a D/s relationship with his business rival.

And yet, they'd had so many security breaches he had to wonder if he wasn't passing up an opportunity.

"You don't think I should go through with it? Maybe it would be a good way to get to know my enemy." And to see if she'd planned it this way. It was too coincidental to think they would be in the same club at the same time and get partnered up in an intimate pairing.

Slaten was known for dirty dealings. Maybe this was her next play. He would never know if he backed off.

Besides, she really was a beautiful woman.

Mitch stared at him in a way that let him know big brother thought he was a dumbass. Flynn wasn't sure how Mitch had perfected that particular stare. It might have come to him naturally when he'd become a dad. "Are you serious?"

It would be better to back off. The trouble with Amy Slaten was her connection to Laurel. Laurel's brother, Will, was married to Bridget, Amy's sister. God, sometimes he was fairly certain any Sanctum family tree would be the weirdest tree, with branches that wound around each other in a stranglehold. He'd managed to stay away from that side of the family. From what he understood, Bridget Slaten, now Daley, took next to no interest in her family company, though she had taken on a voting share when her sister had commandeered Slaten. She would be nothing but a guaranteed vote at a board of directors meeting. He would actually be surprised if Bridget knew who he was and how he was connected to her sister.

"I think it might be interesting to see what happens." And if she'd done all of this so she could play Mata Hari. How far would she go?

Mitch was silent for a moment. A little too silent.

"What aren't you telling me?" Flynn knew when his brother was holding back. Mitch had an incredible poker face, but he rarely used it around his family.

"She might have come in on an assumed name. Not exactly assumed, but she's not using Slaten. She's got her membership under Amy Lyndon. It was her married name, but legally she's gone back to Slaten."

"So she's trying to hide her last name," he mused. "I find that interesting."

"I do too, Flynn." Mitch used his name with a pointed stare. "It's not like you're going in as John, Jr."

Flynn waved that off. "I only went by that at the office. I've always used my middle name since I discovered that chicks dig Irish sounding names. Also, might I point out if I was still using my legal first name, the baby and I would get very confused."

Johnny's head came up at that moment and he yawned as though telling his uncle he didn't have to be confused. He was the center of the universe and he knew it.

Sometimes Flynn kind of envied the kid. He'd never had that kind of attention lavished on him. Not even when he was a baby. He'd had a succession of nannies who came and went. His parents were all right, but they'd led very busy lives and hadn't had time for their children. His father had mellowed over the years and he'd been a much better dad later in life.

Flynn had to face the fact that he was lonely. He'd changed up his life and it had been for the better. He enjoyed his job more now. Chase was happy and healthy. But he'd also isolated himself.

It had been an easy thing to do after how his engagement had ended. He never talked about it. Only Chase knew how he'd screwed up. He hadn't even told Mitch. That was how ashamed he was of not seeing through her lies. After he'd figured out how bad it was, he'd taken a step back and devoted himself to work.

Gaining Master rights at Sanctum had been his way of getting back out there. His brother had introduced him to the lifestyle and he'd realized very quickly it suited him.

That was when he'd started to think about taking a submissive.

It was a logical thing to do. He would look for a woman who wanted the same things he did. They would discuss their relationship up front and work out a contract between them. No more of that shitty go-with-the-flow dating that inevitably ended in him getting his ass kicked. This time he would do it right.

"I thought you were going into this because you were serious about finding a sub." Mitch didn't seem to notice the fact that his son suddenly found his father's nose deeply fascinating. Johnny giggled and he poked at it. "Now you want to play spy?"

"I'm not the one who likes to send in the spies. That's her MO."

"That was her father's MO," Mitch corrected, gently shifting his son so tiny fingers didn't go up his nose. "He and your dad apparently liked to go at it hard. Our dad. Sorry, it's still hard sometimes."

"It's okay." He'd gotten used to Mitch distancing from their father. In some ways, it was a miracle they were so close. Mitch was hard to get to know, but he was loyal once a man was in his circle.

Flynn had earned that. He'd changed his nephew's diapers on occasion. That had to buy him loyalty. Johnny was a cute thing, but he was squirmy and did not skimp on the poop. He was also going to drive his father crazy. Flynn stood and held his hands out. Johnny gleefully went to him.

"I hate that it bothers you," Mitch said, turning back to the dishes and finally making some headway with them. Laurel was working late and Mitch had planned a nice evening for them that included his wife not having to clean the kitchen. "You know I consider you and Chase family. Not consider. You are my family. It's just weird to have gone from having no family to kind of being surrounded by it twenty-four seven."

"Is Daddy feeling suffocated?" Flynn asked Johnny, who drooled and looked ridiculously adorable.

"No," Mitch said with a sigh. "I'm not very good at the advice stuff."

Flynn kept his eyes on the bundle in his hand and shook his head. "But Uncle Flynn didn't ask for advice."

Except he kind of needed it.

"Oh, you asked for it by being a dumbass. I know that much. I've been around enough brothers to know that the first rule of brotherhood is to not let your brother make an ass of himself," Mitch explained.

He had to admit, when Mitch used that tone of voice, he really did feel like the little brother. Sometimes it made him feel oddly welcome. Today it put him on edge. "If she's so innocent, why did we catch a Slaten employee trying to hack into our system?"

Mitch stopped and turned, drying his hands on a towel. "You can prove it?"

Beyond being his brother, Mitch was also a hawk of an attorney. He liked to fly around, looking for places he could swoop in and sue.

"My CEO says he believes it beyond a shadow of a doubt, but you know I can't sue them. I can't even bring the cops into it." The weight of the baby in his arms was soothing. He found himself bouncing on the balls of his feet as Johnny yawned and laid his head on his shoulder.

"Because your stock would tank and we would be viewed as soft." Mitch hung up the towel. "I'm surprised she would do that. You know I advised her on the takeover. I can't talk about it, but I liked her. She seemed very stable and unlike her father. Are we certain this isn't her father still trying to cause trouble? He would likely have people on the inside at Slaten."

Flynn knew well enough that a woman wasn't always as she seemed. "All I know is in the last year, Slaten has come after us and hard, so I find it interesting that a woman who, according to rumors, hates me and my company would end up as my training partner. Oh, but she's not using her real name and she doesn't know I know what she looks like. Does she know I'm your brother?"

"I don't think it's been brought up," Mitch replied. "She only recently moved here and she hasn't done much socializing. Laurel met her briefly at her wedding, but I don't believe they've talked since. Laurel isn't particularly close to Bridget, though they're friendly. We see her at holidays. I assume we'll see Amy with her this year. We'll certainly invite her, but I doubt she's been told anything about you by Laurel."

But Amy knew something. It was the only explanation. "I think this is all one big plan by Slaten. They haven't gotten what they want and now they're sending in the big guns."

"You think they want the code you've been working on?"

Of course they did. "I think they've figured out that I'm working on it remotely so their hackers can't touch it. I've got it on a system with no Internet connection."

He couldn't be too safe. He kept two hard backups, but otherwise he had the only copy of his work.

"As your brother, I'm going to advise you to step back." Mitch walked up and put a hand on his shoulder. "No matter why she's doing it, this isn't business. You can't go into this training relationship without honesty."

That seemed unfair. "I'm not the one who hasn't been honest."

"But you make the choices and decisions when it comes to who you are and what you do to other people. You joined this group to find yourself. Don't turn this into something ugly. Go to the club tonight and explain the situation to Wade. He'll get you into another class and you'll have done the right thing. You can find the relationship you really want. You do the training right and put your heart and soul into it, and I can assure you you'll enjoy yourself. You'll take your time and find the right sub for you. I meant what I said, Flynn. You'll find a lot of peace in the lifestyle if you let it work for you. Laurel and I have."

Yes, Laurel was so submissive. Laurel had actually softened his brother and turned him from a hard-core, full-time Dom into an indulgent husband. He wasn't so sure he was looking for that. The whole marriage ship might have sailed for him. He couldn't trust a woman enough to make that kind of commitment to her, but a contract might do. A well thought out and executed contract with rules and guidelines might bring him some peace.

Was he willing to risk that so he could bring Slaten Industries to…what exactly was his end game with them? They shouldn't compete for clients. Slaten was big, but his firm was gargantuan.

"I'll talk to Wade tonight." He ran his hand over his nephew's back and sighed. Something about a baby…

Maybe it was all about the future. He wanted one. He couldn't have one if he kept getting swept up in the past.

"And I'll set up a meeting with Amy Slaten next week and we'll sit down and hash this out. Like adults. I can go into the next training class and start looking for a sub," Flynn said. "I don't want to play around too much, Mitch. I want something settled."

He wanted a woman who suited him and some peace. That was all. He had his family. It was time to find some happiness and that meant putting the past behind him.

Mitch smiled his way. "I'm so glad to hear you say that."

"Say what?" Laurel walked in the door, followed by Chase.

"Probably something silly." His younger brother was carrying his backpack and some groceries. "Or about code. Flynn loves to talk about code."

Laurel beamed as she kissed Mitch and then turned to her other man. She picked up her son and cuddled him. "Hey, baby boy."

"Flynn was talking sense for once," Mitch said with a smile. "Now I have a lasagna from Top in the fridge. Who wants dinner?"

"I thought you were having quiet time with Laurel." Lasagna sounded ridiculously good and hey, it wasn't like he was going to have a fun night. He got to go into Sanctum and give up his spot and wait another two months for another one.

Two months before his life could start.

He kind of hated Amy Slaten in that moment.

"That's for later," Laurel said with a wink. "Let's have a nice family dinner."

That sounded perfect to Flynn.

Chapter Two

"You're not in leathers, Flynn. Is there a problem? You know I don't teach you how to put them on, right?"

Flynn looked at Wade Rycroft. Sanctum's new Dom in residence was a big man. He probably topped out at six and a half feet.

Flynn liked Wade. He had that ex-military vibe all the McKay-Taggart guys had and for good reason. Wade was a recent refugee from the Green Berets. From what Flynn knew about him, he'd been born in Texas and had come home after he'd been discharged due to injuries sustained in battle.

He was big and scarred and had a ridiculously dark wit.

"I need to talk to you about something." Traffic had made him later than he'd planned. The class was set to start in fifteen minutes.

Wade was dressed in his leathers. Because this was a night class, he wore traditional leathers—pants and vest with boots. No shirt. He looked big and broad. From what Flynn understood, he'd been a cowboy in a past life. He still sent money back to his father's ranch. It was run by his brothers. He wasn't sure how many of them there were, but they were all probably as big as Wade.

Flynn wasn't exactly tiny. When he wasn't working on code, he liked to hit the gym. He could walk into any place and feel comfortable in his own skin. He was a little bitter he wasn't walking into the dungeon tonight. He could be starting that part of his life.

But no. Someone wanted to play games. Again, he kind of hated her. If she hadn't brought their war to the dungeon, he might be meeting a pretty sub this very evening.

Wade held up a hand. "Can you wait a second? I need to make sure I'm properly set up for tonight's class. It's my first training class without a Taggart breathing down my neck. Don't want to disappoint. I'll be right back."

He stepped away and Flynn was left in the hallway that connected the locker rooms to the lounge and bar. They would have to go upstairs to reach the dungeon.

Sanctum was the Cadillac of dungeons. Three stories of pure luxury kink that he would have to wait to indulge in.

The door to the women's locker room came open and he heard feminine laughter. It was light and airy and made him realize it had been far too long since his last date. He'd pulled away from so much in the last few years. Between his doomed engagement and his father's death, he'd gotten so fucking serious. He'd had to be a father to Chase and keep the company running. He'd felt so damn old the last couple of years. He wanted to feel like he was in his prime. Which according to the media and other sources, he was.

He didn't feel that way.

Three women stepped out, each lovely in her own way. They were all dressed in fet wear of some kind, two in corsets and miniskirts and one in a tight tank and leather boy shorts. No bra and he could see the outline of her nipples.

Normally he would glance away, but Sanctum was different from the outside world.

He gave them a tip of his head. "Ladies, you are all looking lovely tonight."

"Thank you, Sir," one said.

Her friend shook her head. "How do you know he's a Sir? He could be a sub, too. Men can be subs."

The third one grinned as if this was all one big adventure for her. "He looks like a Dom to me."

But he wasn't yet and it looked like it would be another few months before he could take the class. It was a shame because he'd already been through the Dom training portion. The classes were segregated in the beginning. Doms learned how to behave from Doms and subs had a class of their own. This was the last step to gaining access to club membership.

"Enjoy your class, ladies." He winked their way and then sighed as they strode up the stairs, perfectly confident in themselves. "I know Wade will take care of you."

One of those lovely women might have been his training sub if Amy Slaten hadn't wrecked everything.

"Hi, I know this is probably not a request you get a lot, but is there any way you could help me finish zipping this sucker up?"

He turned and there was a woman poking her head from behind the wall that led back to the women's locker room. She gave him a heart-stopping grin.

"There's a hug in it for you at the end," she promised. "Or a hearty fist bump. Really, it's whichever makes you more comfortable. I'd offer you candy, but then I would be the creepy chick who walks around offering strange Doms candy. And that would be bad. And I am talking too much. It's this thing I do when I get nervous. I talk a lot. Like now."

He couldn't help but smile. She was standing in the shadows, but he could see her broad smile and it did something for him.

Damn, but he liked a funny girl. He'd always liked the weird ones, the slightly nerdy awkward goddess ones did him in time and time again.

"I would never refuse a damsel in distress." He stepped up and stopped.

Now he could plainly see her. Pretty blue eyes, a ridiculous amount of shiny black hair, and lips that looked like they'd been made to kiss. Those lips were plump and bountiful. She was tall and had a slender grace that reminded him of a doe.

Ah, the wolf in sheep's clothing. Amy Slaten was standing right there, already trying to pull him in.

"Thank you so much," she said with a sigh. She turned around, presenting her back to him. Her corset had a zipper in the back, unlike the lace-up ones most subs used. She'd managed to get it about halfway up. "I thought I could get one of the other women to help me with it, but I took a shower when I got here so I would smell nice and apparently I took too long and all the other women were gone. You know it's a little weird in there when no one else is around. I might have watched one too many horror movies. The chick who takes the shower always gets murdered. You would think they have something against cleanliness."

For a slender girl, she had a lovely backside. It was round and perfect and looked amazing in boy shorts, where he could see the under curves of her ass.

She held her hair, piling it high on her head. It had grown out since the last time he'd seen her. The bob she'd had it in was now long and would likely brush her shoulder blades. So much hair. He would be able to twist his hand in it and command her.

"If it bothers you, I can find someone else." She suddenly didn't sound as sure as she had before.

He stepped up and reached for the zipper. "Not at all. I'm sorry."

"It's okay. I don't want to offend anyone. At first I was thinking you were probably staring at my ass because that is totally on display, but then you were so quiet that I was worried maybe you were offended by my ass being on display, and that was when I realized you're not in leathers and you could be the repair guy here to plug in a few light bulbs, and crazy pants with her ass hanging out is suddenly asking for you to zip her up."

He did exactly that, but it was a tight fit, molding to her every curve, and he had to put a hand on her waist to balance it and get the zipper up. The curve of her hip fit perfectly in his hand and he could smell the citrus of her shampoo. "I was absolutely looking at your ass and no, it did not offend me. It's quite lovely, as is the rest of you. I'm not the repairman."

Her head turned slightly and he was captivated by the line of her jaw, the way her lips curled up. "I'm glad to hear that. So you're in the class? Or are you teaching the class?"

This was the point in time that he explained he wasn't taking the class because he wasn't going to allow her to drag out some years old feud between their families. This was the moment when he explained to her who he was and that her game wasn't going to work on him and better luck next time, baby. Try again. Yes, this was when he turned her around and faced her and said thanks but no thanks. I'm an adult and I don't play games.

"I'm in training, too."

She turned and he got a good look at the front of her. Unfortunately, it was just as hot as the back. Her breasts fit into the corset like a dream. They weren't large, but they looked perfect for her. For him. They would likely fit right in the palm of his hand.

She winked at him, her hair tumbling around her shoulders. "You should probably change then. I've heard the punishment for Doms who are late can only be applied with the proper amount of lube."

He frowned. "Are you serious?"

He'd already been through that part. He didn't want to do that again. Not to himself. To her though…

Her eyes lit with mirth. "Oh, I hope I get you. You would be so much fun to tease, Sir."

"And you would be a lot of fun to spank, sub," he said, his voice deepening because she was pushing all the right buttons to bring out the Dom in him. The one who wanted to play. He actually didn't mind her teasing him. He didn't want a sub who never spoke unless she was spoken to or one who obeyed him mindlessly.

Fuck, he should have known he would want the brat.

Her eyes went down submissively, but he caught the smile on her face. "Yes, Sir. I look forward to it. Thank you so much for the help. I appreciate it. So fist bump or hug?"

"I would rather have a kiss." Who the hell was talking? He was pretty sure it was his dick. The damn thing seemed to have taken firm control of the body and it was not letting the brain in. Why should it? The brain couldn't function when all the available blood supply had gone straight to his cock.

Her eyes widened and he felt a thrill go through his system. She thought she had the upper hand? He wouldn't touch her without her permission, but in a club like this it was totally acceptable to ask as long as he did it politely. He could ask her if she'd like to go upstairs to one of the privacy rooms with him so he could fuck her long and hard. All she had to do was say no.

Communication was the key. Saying what he wanted and what he was and wasn't willing to give.

Honesty is pretty important, too, asshole. Communication means nothing without honesty.

His brain was still functioning on some level. Maybe if she turned him down flat he could still get out of this.

And then she stepped up. The heels she was wearing gave her a few inches, but she had to look up at him, her eyes softening as she got close. She went up on her toes and put her hands on either side of his face. She stared at him for a moment, but it wasn't odd or uncomfortable. He got the feeling she was memorizing him or being truly in the moment. For a second he forgot about everything that was happening and looked at her, studying the angles and planes of her lovely face. Her lips had taken him, but now he was utterly fascinated by the freckles sprinkled across the bridge of her nose and the tiny scar on her left cheek.

Then she moved up, pressing her lips to his. It was only a moment, but heat flashed through his system and he was more alive in that second than he'd felt in years.

She moved down again, her hands coming to her sides and her lips curling up slightly. "Thank you, Sir. I'll see you upstairs."

His hands fisted. He wanted to touch her, to drag her back and show her how to properly kiss her Master.

He was a fucking fool and he would never learn.

"I didn't get your name," he heard himself saying.

Please tell me the truth. Give me your name. Your real name. Let me believe this was all a crazy coincidence and you're not playing me.

She turned back slightly as she moved toward the stairs. "It's Amy. Amy Lyndon. How about you, Sir?"

Something inside him went cold. Unfortunately, it was not his dick. "Flynn."

"Is that your first name or last name?"

Two could play at her game. She knew damn well what his name was. "It's John Flynn, but I prefer Flynn."

No lies there. Merely a set of truths withheld, but then she'd done the same to him.

"It was nice to meet you. I hope...well, I hope you enjoy the class." She walked up the stairs.

"Damn, you work fast, Flynn." Wade stepped down the stairs after he nodded to Amy. "I think Kai was right on with that pick. Sorry, it was supposed to be a surprise. She's your training sub. Sweet lady. I already like her. She's funny, and I would bet she'll give you plenty of excuses to smack that pretty ass. She's in this for the adventure of it. Those are my favorites."

She'd worked fast. She'd turned him upside down and inside out with nothing more than a few words and an undone zipper.

And there was absolutely no way he was walking out now.

"Good. I think that should make the class very interesting," Flynn said, his eyes still on her. He kept watching her until she disappeared.

"You wanted to talk to me about something?" Wade asked.

Flynn shook his head. "Nah, it was nothing. I'll go change."

"You better hurry," Wade said with a frown. "You know what happens to Doms who are late to my class."

It didn't involve lube but it wasn't pretty. "I'll be on time."

He wasn't about to miss it. It was the start of their game.

He intended to win.

* * * *

What the hell had she done? Amy managed to walk sedately up the stairs. She was pretty sure he was still watching her.

Him. Flynn.

God, she was blushing at the very thought of him. He was some kind of actor or model. He had to be because that man was flipping gorgeous. He was tall and broad and she'd kissed him.

I would rather have a kiss.

Her heart had threatened to flatline then and there. He'd said it in a low growl that had gone straight past her ears to her female parts, and she'd found herself doing something crazy. She'd gone up on her toes and kissed him but not before she'd really looked at him. There was something about the man, something in his eyes. Something that called to her.

Flynn.

Flynn.

She liked Flynn better than John. Way better. She already had one too many Johns in her world.

What was she doing? She'd already kissed a Dom, and one who was in her training class. How was she going to feel when he got paired up with another sub?

She looked up ahead at the dungeon space they'd designated as the classroom for the night. It looked like there were four women and three men up ahead. She'd known it was a small class, but then Sanctum was pretty selective from what she understood. They tended to take in new members by referral only. She was here because of her sister.

Who did Flynn know?

Maybe he worked for McKay-Taggart. The club had founded around a group of ex-military men who formed a security company. It had been completely private for years, but now they were taking new members since they had a much bigger space.

Apparently the last space had blown up.

Maybe she didn't want him working for McKay-Taggart. They had dangerous jobs. Maybe he was someone's brother and he had a perfectly normal, didn't get shot on a regular basis job.

She didn't want him to get shot. She kind of wanted to kiss him again.

Focus. She needed to focus on the task at hand and that was not making a complete idiot of herself in front of the class.

She wished she'd talked more to the other subs. The prep class hadn't been held on the dungeon floor. It had been done in the downstairs conference room and it had mostly been a lecture about safety. They'd been allowed to familiarize themselves with the equipment and explore the club. She'd spent the majority of her time talking to the woman who had led the class. Kori Williamson was engaged to the psychologist who'd approved them all for entrance. Unlike her very serious husband-to-be, Kori was fun and didn't seem to mind that she sometimes talked way too much.

Kori wasn't here today and she hadn't gotten to know the other three women.

She put on a smile. She wouldn't admit it but she was shy. One didn't run a company and get to indulge her shyness. Her father had seen it as a weakness and done whatever he could to ruthlessly purge it from her. So she knew how to put on a confident smile even when she kind of wanted to run away. She pretty much felt that way at every board meeting and she knew all those fuckers.

The three women were standing to the side, whispering among themselves. There was a full complement of hair colors. The tall one was blonde and built like a swimsuit model. There was a petite redhead with a sweet smile and a curvy body, and a brunette who looked a bit like she should be standing with the Doms. She was on the severe side. If she had to guess, that woman likely worked for the security company. She had a military look about her.

The redhead gave her a wave. "Hi, Amy."

Amy searched her memory. Redhead, she'd worn lace the first day but it hadn't been racy. Lucy. "Hi, Lucy." She glanced at the other two. They'd all been introduced that first class. Blonde like Dolly Parton. Jolene. "Jolie, it's nice to see you again." Brunette. Held herself like a queen. "Regina."

Regina frowned. "How do you remember everyone's names? Did you write them down? Because I didn't write them down and I haven't talked to you at all. I don't remember your name and now I feel bad about it. I don't like feeling bad about things."

Jolie sighed. "Don't mind her. She's nervous. She doesn't like feeling nervous either. I'm pretty sure she doesn't like feeling much of anything."

"Emotions are overrated," Regina agreed.

"I use a mnemonic device," Amy explained, grateful to be talking. "It's one of those things they teach you when they're training you to be in sales."

Lucy nodded. "My dad was a salesman. Insurance. He had to go into a room full of people and memorize names very quickly."

"I can never remember names," Jolie complained. "But I think I want to memorize that man's abs. I'm sorry. We were objectifying the men. Want to join us? Any idea why there are four of us and only three of them?"

"I'm not sharing," Regina said. "I did that enough during my marriage. I told Karina this wouldn't work. I'm not a ménage girl. Not if there's another girl involved. I don't like girls. I definitely don't want to share a Dom with one."

"I met the fourth one downstairs." She was with Regina. She kind of didn't want to share either. Not Flynn. It wasn't her call. "I think there are enough to go around."

"I don't know. I think that one is totally big enough to share." Lucy was eyeing the biggest guy in the room, a massive slab of muscle.

"I've actually seen him before. He comes into the restaurant I work at every now and then. I think they call him Bear. Or is that one of those mnemonic devices?"

"That was his call sign in the military, ladies," a deep voice said. Suddenly Wade was behind them, staring them all down. "Do I need to go over the club rules on gossip?"

The other three were quiet, though Regina was silent with a mulish look on her face. Lucy and Jolie suddenly seemed to find their feet really interesting.

So it was up to her. Every group of subs needed a ringleader. She'd learned that from Bridget's books. It looked like that was going to be her. "We weren't gossiping, Sir."

Wade turned on her like a predator who'd recently figured out where his next meal was going to come from. "Then what were you doing, sub?"

Yep. All eyes were on her now. Awesome. Regina's lips curled up in a snarky smile as if to say, yeah, newbie, get us all out of this one.

All the men were looking at her, including the truly gorgeous one who looked even better in leathers than he had in street clothes. Flynn joined the other men and damn but that boy worked out. He also had the steely-eyed thing down. He was staring at her, waiting for her answer.

There was nothing to do but answer him honestly. "We were objectifying them, Sir. Sexually."

A laugh exploded out of Wade's mouth but he quickly covered it by coughing. He shook his head as though that had been the last thing he'd been expecting. She could see the baby Doms all smiling.

With the exception of one. Flynn did not look amused.

Wade's lips were still curled up, though his shoulders squared. "Ladies, these are men and they have feelings. You can not treat them like sexual objects."

"I would like to be treated as a sexual object, darlin'," the tall, lean one with sandy blonde hair said. "Don't you listen to the big bad Dom. You objectify away."

Wade rolled his eyes. "Let this be a lesson. Never ever let your brother talk you into being his training Dom. I'm already uncomfortable. Let's get started. Once you've been partnered, I would like you to take the first few minutes of this class to talk to your partner about what you're looking for from training. Over the next few days, you'll develop your contract and begin to figure out how you work as partners. Rand, you are partnered with Jolie. Please go and sit down and try not to act like a dumbass."

Rand strode forward and held a hand out to the lovely blonde. "Don't listen to him, darlin'. He's just irritated because I got all the looks in the family."

Jolie was smiling as she walked toward the set of chairs that had been placed in the "classroom."

Wade simply shook his head as he looked down at his clipboard. "Vaughn is a new McKay-Taggart employee. He works with the personal security unit, but he comes from LAPD. I think you'll have a lot in common with Regina. She's DPD."

Regina's eyes went wide as the very muscular Vaughn stepped up. Amy could practically see the tough cop arguing in her head that this was all wrong and she should walk out right now.

Amy leaned over. "Oh, you can totally take him. I'm backing you in that fight."

Regina's jaw tightened and the slightest spark hit her eyes. "You better. Hello. I'm Regina."

Vaughn nodded her way as though he got she wasn't ready for anything touchy feely. "Vaughn. Good to meet you. I take it you're one of Brighton's?"

"He's my CO, but I'm good friends with his wife, who's pretty much the most kick ass chick I've ever met," she was saying as they walked away.

Two down. Two to go. Flynn was still standing across from her, his eyes intent. Was he thinking the same thing? Was he hoping she was his partner? Or was he praying Wade called out Lucy's name with his?

She wasn't normally insecure about her looks, but Lucy was petite and curvy, with a healthy rack. If Flynn was into big boobs—and most men were—he would probably prefer Lucy.

Or he might have totally changed his mind and decided she was a mouthy brat. Which she very likely was and then it would be for the best that they weren't together because she wasn't going to change that.

She intended to be respectful and follow the rules they agreed on, but if he didn't like a little snark, she wasn't the sub for him.

"Lucy, my dear, you've been paired with Bear, who has a very good story about his name," Wade continued. "And that leaves Flynn and our resident brat. I call you that because you're going to be trouble and now everyone knows it."

Flynn stepped up, his face grim. "Nice to see you again, Amy."

Wow, that seemed like it was so not nice to see her again. Damn it. Her mouth got her in trouble time and time again.

Lucy and Bear walked toward the chairs with Wade and she was left standing alone with a man she'd kissed not ten minutes before. She'd felt so close to him in that moment. Like they'd connected.

Not so now.

And she was stuck with him for six weeks.

"Nice to see you, too." She flashed a smile. Cry on the inside, girl. "So we're partners."

"Apparently."

So he was big on conversation. Maybe this was his Dom space. She'd been told some Doms changed when they walked onto a dungeon floor. They took on harsher personas. If he was this cold, she was in for a very chilly month and a half.

God, she'd hoped for some warmth.

"Should we join the others?" Maybe he would warm up once he got to know her. They could talk. Maybe he was as nervous as she was and instead of talking like an idiot, he got cold and unapproachable.

"We're fine."

She stood for a moment and for the first time she felt self-conscious about what she was wearing. She hadn't minded at all earlier. She'd felt pretty. The way he was looking at her made her reassess.

And that kind of made her mad. This was supposed to be a safe place for her.

"Is there something I can do for you, Sir?" If he was cold, she could be, too. This was only a training class. She had to get through it to get to the good stuff. If she got stuck with an asshole Dom for six weeks, then she could handle it. She'd survived eighteen years in the home of a man who couldn't stand her. She could handle this asshole for a brief period of time.

"You can explain to me why you're here."

It felt like a drill sergeant questioning a wayward recruit. Sir. Yes, Sir and all that. She straightened her posture, her spine becoming rigid. She'd done it all her life when she felt threatened. "I want to explore the lifestyle, Sir."

"From what I heard a moment ago, I think you're just looking to get laid."

She stared him straight in the eyes because she wasn't putting up with that and he needed to understand right now. "I'm here to explore my sexuality. That very likely means I will end up sleeping with someone. I would enjoy it if the partner was right. I thought this was the place I could do that without judgment. If I'm wrong and Sanctum has its double standards like the rest of the world, then please, Sir, let me know now so I can go home to my vibrator. His name is Oliver and he doesn't judge me."

"You're very forthright."

"I thought that would be to my advantage." He wasn't the only Dom in the sea. Still, she didn't want to lose this opportunity. If she simply walked away she would have to explain it all to that big Taggart guy and he kind of scared her. She'd come here to have fun and maybe make some friends and not have to be the ball buster she had to be in her daily life. The last thing she wanted to do was put that off for another six weeks. "Look, I can easily see that you're disappointed. I'm sorry you feel that way, but I doubt they'll change the pairings. How about we sit down and make a deal? I want this chance. It's six weeks. You only have to see me here in the club. I'll be obedient and you'll be respectful and we'll get through the class."

"There are homework portions to the class," he argued. "And evenings we'll be expected to spend together here at Sanctum."

He wasn't bending and she didn't feel like charming him. She was so sick of having to maneuver her way through every second of the day. It was one of the things that appealed to her about D/s. There wasn't supposed to be a ton of bullshit, but it looked like she'd stepped into it again.

She shoved aside her softer self and put on her CEO hat. Get things done. Even when the task was unpleasant.

"You don't think you can stand to be around me for six weeks? I find that a bit arrogant when you know nothing about me. It appears to me you've already judged me and found me lacking. I don't understand it. Maybe it's your way of getting the upper hand. I believe you'll find humiliation was one of my hard limits, Flynn. I'll have a talk with Wade after class and explain the situation to him. Good luck."

She turned to go. She would get dressed and have a long talk with Wade. There were things she couldn't put up with. They'd chosen improperly for her. She couldn't stand any man who had no warmth.

But he'd seemed so warm before. So giving.

Maybe that was how he trapped his prey.

"I was jealous."

She sighed and turned. "Jealous of what?"

His cheeks had a slight flush. "You objectifying the other men. It bugged me and I know that it's stupid because we've known each other for less than an hour."

"I made a joke," she stated flatly because that wasn't an excuse. Not a good enough one. "And you made me feel like shit because of it. Is that the way you handle things when you're jealous?"

"I don't get jealous." His voice had softened and he stepped toward her. That hard stance he'd taken relaxed a bit as his shoulders eased down. "I haven't felt that way since I was a kid, Amy, and I didn't handle it well. I'm sorry. I had an emotional response and I haven't had one of those in a very long time."

If they could be civil she would greatly prefer to take the class. As soon as it was over, she didn't have to be close to Flynn again. She didn't want a jealous jerk in her life. "I'm not something to possess or to punch when you're feeling bad. I flirted with you pretty hard downstairs. Hell, I was excited about the potential of you being my partner. I did not like how you made me feel so let me apologize for flirting."

His face fell. "Can we please start over again?"

Not until she'd made a few things clear to him. "I've been batted around all my life, Flynn. I'm not going to take it from a man I barely know. I need you to understand that if we're working together, you can't do that to me again. You do it again and I will walk away."

"Hard limit," he said with a nod. "How about I take a fist bump this time and we slow down?" He moved in and brought his hand up, his thumb swiping across her cheek. "Amy, I'm very sorry. I didn't mean to make you cry. Please forgive me and know I won't do it again."

He sounded so sincere. And why did she have to cry? She thought she'd purged that from her system a long time ago.

She nodded. "So maybe we can be friends."

He held a hand out. "Friends who see each other mostly naked."

She had to smile at that. She shook his hand. "All right."

It was a start.

Chapter Three

"What happened to 'I'm going to talk to Wade, Mitch? I'm going to do the right thing and end this fiasco before it begins'?"

His brother didn't even wait for the elevator doors to close behind him. He was yelling as he got off the private elevator that led to Flynn's penthouse. He was dressed for work and still carrying his briefcase, a sure sign that he hadn't even stopped at home before coming over for this particular lecture.

Flynn winced inwardly. He hadn't exactly gotten around to telling his brother that the whole walking away from Amy Slaten thing hadn't happened. It had been a full week and he'd managed to avoid this conversation altogether.

Now he was a little worried he was about to get found out.

Next week he would have his first night at Sanctum with his training sub at his side. He'd gotten his pick of nights and he'd selected Thursday because Mitch and Laurel didn't play on Thursdays. He'd hedged his bets. Amy's sister, Bridget, was on bed rest so he wouldn't have issues there. He wasn't sure the rest of the Daley clan would even know him by name. Everyone else at Sanctum had no idea that Amy and he owned companies that were involved in a feud. Oh, he was certain Big Tag had some understanding of it because the big guy seemed to know everything, but he wouldn't come up and ask questions about it.

Mitch might be another story.

"She's different than I thought she'd be." Flynn had spent the five classes they'd had studying her mostly. Sure, they'd gone over contracts and how to behave in the club and started to explore the equipment, but mostly he'd watched her.

"Different how?"

He shrugged. "I don't know. She's funny. She's kind of weird."

He liked her weird. That talking thing she did always amused him. Her stream of consciousness commentary when she got nervous led her in odd directions. Before the spanking class she'd spent fifteen minutes talking about how she'd read about spanking but had never actually had one before, and somehow she'd ended making a statement about snowflakes.

He found her fascinating.

Mitch sat his briefcase down on the bar. "Weird?"

How did he explain this? "She's not the girl I thought she would be. She's open and funny and weird. Like quirky weird. She has quirks."

He'd expected a tight-assed Type A. Since that first day in training class, he'd looked into her a bit. Nothing more than reading her bio. And finding pictures of her and the ex. Now that he didn't expect. The ex looked like a flipping male model.

He was surprised at how strongly jealous he could be about her. He'd been a complete ass that first day. He'd walked up those stairs and she'd been talking about objectifying the other guys and they'd all been leering at her. Maybe not leering, but definitely looking and admiring and it had bugged the holy fuck out of him.

He'd been engaged. He'd asked a woman to marry him, helped her plan a whole wedding, and when he'd found out she was marrying him for money and had a lover on the side, he'd very calmly broken everything off. Oh, he'd been angry, but it had been a controlled burn.

What he'd felt for Amy hadn't been controlled. It had been a flash fire and he'd behaved like a fucking caveman. He'd almost lost her.

He still wasn't sure what the hell he was doing, but he felt more alive than he had in a very long time so he was kind of going with it.

He was careful. They met at the club for class and they'd had dinner a few times afterward. They'd talked about innocuous things. She liked baseball and watched an enormous amount of science fiction and fantasy shows. He'd been shocked at that fact. Outside the club and in street clothes she looked very much like the type of woman who would run a company. Her clothes were all designer and flattering, but they reminded him of armor. She didn't look like a girl who had watched every episode of *Star Trek*.

The truth was he was pretty geeky himself. His tastes ran to superheroes. Normally he tried to hide that fact, but Amy just put it all out there. She loved a show called *Dart* that he followed too, and they seemed to have similar tastes in movies. They'd passed a very pleasant evening talking about *Doctor Who*.

He liked her. He had to face that fact. Maybe she was the single smartest woman in the world and she knew how to play him on every level, or maybe she simply was who she was. He needed more time to sort it out.

He needed more time because he wanted so desperately to get back to that place where she stared up at him like he was something to memorize right before she kissed him.

"Everyone has quirks," Mitch shot back. "I'm the quirkiest motherfucker on the planet but that doesn't mean anyone should risk their business reputation to sleep with me. I assume you're already sleeping with her."

His brother was an optimist. She'd been sweet and friendly, but he'd fucked up that first day.

Shouldn't she have forgiven him much more quickly if insinuating herself into his life had been the plan all along? Should she have taken his jealousy and used it against him? Instead she'd told him to fuck off.

Had that been calculated, too?

"As a matter of fact, we're not sleeping together," he said as he closed the lid to his laptop. He should have known his brother would figure it out. It wasn't like he could hide it forever.

But he had to admit, it had been nice for a while. It had felt intimate, like he had a secret. Like they'd been the only two who knew what was going on.

He kind of liked playing this game with her. He'd started to wonder if she hadn't done this so she could get to know him. Maybe if she came to care about him, she would back off and figure out they didn't have to be enemies.

Stranger things had happened.

Mitch sighed. "You want to explain to me what you're doing then? Because if you're playing her, it's going to blow back on me with my friends. Big Tag will have issues with you using a training relationship for some kind of revenge plot. If she's playing you, it could have very bad ramifications to Glendale and we're both heavily invested. Chase is, too."

"I'm not playing her. I'm still trying to figure out if she's playing me. I'm kind of starting to believe she's not. Do you think it's possible she's feeling me out? Like she wants to get to know me?"

Mitch seemed to visibly calm, his face turning curious. "Is that what you're doing? Getting to know her?"

He had no fucking idea what he was doing. "Maybe."

"What has she told you about herself?"

There was the rub. "She said she works for a big corporation. She told me it was too boring to go into. When I try to talk about her work, she diverts me."

"Does she ask about your work?"

"Yes. I told her I worked for McKay-Taggart writing code for their security systems."

A long sigh issued from Mitch. "And you say you're not playing her."

"I'm feeling her out. I think that's what we're both doing. And I do write code and I have been working with Chelsea Weston on a security system code."

Mitch settled himself on the couch across from Flynn. "I know you do and it's important code. That's why I'm worried. Have you talked to your CEO today? Do you know what's going on?"

He felt himself frown. "I got some texts but I was busy."

"You're not paying enough attention to the business," his brother chided.

"Do you have any idea how much you sound like our father right now?" Big brother was taking on their father's persona in his old age.

Mitch sent him his happy middle finger. "Dad ever do that?"

"Our father was actually quite proper and uptight, so no. I never saw him shoot anyone the bird," Flynn admitted. "You know you could take over the company. I would one hundred percent give that job to you. He left you stock."

"Yes, which I offered to give back to you and Chase," Mitch pointed out. "I'll oversee legal, but I'm happiest working for myself. Have you considered selling?"

Only a million times. He could take the money and use it to start his own tech business. "I can't until I'm sure Chase won't want to take over. I'm keeping it solid until he's old enough to make an informed decision. He needs to get through college and then we'll talk. Until then, the guy I hired to run the company is solid."

"He's a ruthless shark with five rows of razor sharp teeth," Mitch pointed out.

"Yes, so he'll take care of the company. He's being paid a nominal salary. His real money comes in bonuses if he meets the company growth goals." It was the way CEOs got paid in his world.

"He called me an hour ago, which is another reason I'm here. He couldn't get you on the phone. He said he got a call from a man who used to work for Slaten. He's willing to talk for a fee."

"Talk? About what?" His stomach tightened. He didn't want to discuss this. It was so much easier to pretend Amy was nothing more than his training partner and a girl he was trying to get into bed. He was happier with that Amy. They were rapidly becoming friends.

He hadn't had one of those in a very long time.

"About Slaten and their business practices," Mitch said with a frown. "He says he knows the ins and outs like no one else and he can prove that Slaten has been sending in corporate spies for years. He claims there are still a few. He's also willing to talk about their upcoming bids."

"And he used to work for Slaten?"

"He was fired by Amy about a week after she took over the company. You know new CEOs like to clean house."

They tended to want their own people in the power positions. "How many people did Amy fire when she took over?"

"Her father's entire management team."

He'd hoped to hear something different. "It's not unusual."

"Her father was a genuinely terrible human being. He still is. There was a reason I helped her with the takeover."

"Did she enjoy the fact that you were her rival's son?"

Mitch sighed. "It didn't come up. It was more of a favor for

Bridget than anything. And the asshole pissed off Big Tag. You know Ian lives to fuck with people who piss him off. She was likely very smart to fire everyone. She gave them packages. Only her father and this guy sued her."

"So the man who's suing her is coming to us to sell her out?" Well, that was about as shady as it got. "I'll call Curt and tell him I don't want to have anything to do with the man."

The decision made him feel good. He wasn't going to fall into that trap.

Was it a trap?

Mitch's eyes narrowed. "Is this like what you said about talking to Wade and I'm going to go home and the dude will have moved in with you tomorrow?"

A guy makes one little course correction and he's got sarcasm forever. "No, I'll call him right now. Do you see me? This is me calling."

He picked up his cell and hit the button that would connect him with his CEO, Curt Hamilton. It was to his personal line so Flynn didn't have to go through either of the two assistants the man kept with him at all times.

"Adler, I thought I was going to have to call the troops in to find you," a deep voice said over the line.

"You did. Mitch is here."

He chuckled. "Well. Trust the lawyer to get things done for once. Did he explain the situation to you? The man's name is Ray Paulsen and he's legit. I've checked into his background and he really did work for Slaten for years. Apparently he ran afoul of the daughter. She's a ball-busting bitch according to him."

"Hey, don't talk about her that way." His anger flared.

"What?"

"How about we keep the sexual harassment to a minimum and just say she's tough?" He couldn't explain to his CEO that he was kind of involved with their biggest rival and now he wanted to punch Curt's nose through the back of his face because he'd called her a bitch. She wasn't a bitch. She was tough and smart. That made her good in his book.

Unless she was setting him up. It occurred to him that planting someone like this Paulsen guy could put them in a bad position. He could also say anything he wanted, feeding them false information and causing chaos. If the employees knew there was a spy hunt, it could demoralize the entire company and they would lose some of their best talent.

It would be a sneaky play.

"Ray Paulsen is also suing her," Flynn stated flatly. The jury was still out on whether this was a ploy of Amy's or her way of figuring him out. He wasn't sure and he wasn't going to push it. Things were going well between them right now. Eventually he was going to sit her down and explain that he'd known who she was all along and they needed to come to an agreement on how to end this feud.

If she wasn't here to take the fight to a whole different level.

"That's not on us," Curt replied. "That's on him. He's the one who stands to lose. Listen, let me put him on the payroll for a few weeks and see what shakes out. I'll talk to him and that's all it has to be. We gather some information and find out what's happening over there. Consider it a fact finding mission."

He made it sound so reasonable. "No. We don't need spies."

"You're joking, right? Tell me you're not that naïve, Flynn. You do understand two of the people she fired after she took over had been plants from your father. He knew what it took to do business these days."

He'd known his father was ruthless. "I'm not my dad. I don't want to play like that."

"So you're willing to let Slaten send spies in here. Look, we're in the middle of negotiations to buy a company that will make your pet project work, right? If we can't get the infrastructure to ensure we're capable of selling that software, it's utterly useless."

He didn't need a lecture. "I expect you to be smart enough to buy the company. What can Slaten do?"

"Slaten can find out what our bid is and outbid us," Curt pointed out. "They can do any number of things. If there's a spy on the team negotiating they can tank the entire process. Look, I called you as a courtesy to let you know what I'm planning on doing. I've got an ironclad contract so unless you want to pay me my salary and the guaranteed ten million you'll owe me if you fire me, you should let me do my job."

"Is he strong-arming you?" Mitch asked, his loafer tapping against the marble floor. "Because we can get rid of him."

For a ton of money and he would have to go back to California and run the damn thing himself while he put on another exhaustive search for a CEO. He would have to leave the training program.

He would have to leave Amy and he wouldn't have the chance to figure her out. Wasn't that meaningful, too?

If he wanted to go up against the CEO, he would have to get the board together and they would have to vote. A no confidence vote against Hamilton could potentially trigger his contract based on whether it was on philosophy or incompetence.

If the board would vote his way. The board was still from his father's era. They would likely be all for Hamilton's maneuvers.

Frustration welled inside him. It was his fucking company and he was in a corner. "You be careful with this. Do you understand me?"

A sigh of blatant relief came over the line. "I'm going to let security handle it, and if Mitch wants to come over and talk to Paulsen himself, I think that might be a good idea. He's got a great sense for telling bullshit from the truth. I'm not trying to cause trouble here. I know you're sensitive to the way your dad conducted business, but he was right to treat Slaten like an enemy. I don't think you understand how far the Slatens were willing to go to fuck with your dad."

"Do you know why? My father never talked about it with me." It was a mystery to him.

"I think it was personal. The rumors are at one point your father might have embarrassed Slaten or something. He held a grudge and it looks like his daughter is carrying on the family tradition."

There were still problems with Hamilton's plan. "Paulsen's a disgruntled employee. I don't think we can count on him to be honest about the woman who fired him."

"Flynn, I know that you want to be an idealist and stay above the fray. That's precisely why you hired me. I also know that eventually you're going to want to sell this company and start your own. Let me do my job. Let me get you the best price we can get so you can start with more than enough money to be the businessman you want to be. I knew your father. He would want that for you. He had to get down in the mud and fight it out so you wouldn't have to."

The man was saying all the right things. "Like I said, be careful. Send me an update."

He hung up the phone.

Mitch groaned. "This is why I don't want to run that fucking company. Look, how do you want to handle this? If you're unhappy with Hamilton, we pay him and get his ass out of here. I can get the board votes for you."

He was so close to beta testing his software. So fucking close. It would be exactly what Hamilton had said. If they could get the infrastructure in place, they could sell it and then everyone would make a ton of money. If Chase wanted to run the company, Flynn would pass it happily off to him. If he didn't, Flynn would likely have enough money that he could be free.

"He says you can come up and talk to him," Flynn explained. "He's going to be careful. He says this guy might know something about what Slaten is planning in the next few months."

"And if he's lying?"

"At least we'll know we looked into it." He was suddenly tired. "Is he right? Am I being idealistic?"

"Probably, but you have good intentions. Look, keep those good intentions going with Amy. You like the girl. That's obvious. She's not her father, but that doesn't mean she won't do what it takes to protect her business and it also doesn't mean she's not somewhere sitting in her office and having to listen to a million different voices telling her what to do. Just like you are. She's got a board to answer to and I'm not sure they're in the best position financially right now. I can say that because it's merely an opinion. I'm no longer her advisor in any way. But I watch the markets and I listen. Her father isn't giving up. He's hell-bent on causing trouble. Amy's got to prove her worth or that board will oust her."

"You think she wants to prove her worth by taking our contracts?"

He shrugged. "I don't know. Why don't you ask her?"

There was a very good reason for that. "Because the minute I do that, I can no longer learn anything about her. Right now she thinks I don't know who she is."

"Does it matter? You can't negotiate with her unless you're

honest."

"This is more than fucking business, Mitch." The words exploded in a wave of frustration. Damn it. He hadn't meant to admit that. Not really.

"You want her."

He turned and stared out the ceiling-to-floor glass windows. They offered him a phenomenal view of the city. At night he could swear he was all alone in the world.

He didn't want to be alone anymore and that wasn't strictly about being lonely. He wanted her.

"I think I could care about her, but I need time."

"All right," Mitch conceded, "but I'm going to look into this and I'm going to oversee everything Hamilton does."

His cell phone trilled. He frowned as he realized it was the number for the Dallas Police Department. His stomach flipped and he prayed Chase wasn't in trouble again. He'd done so well for so long.

He picked it up and slid his thumb across the screen to accept. "Hello?"

"Flynn, I'm in trouble. Can you help me?" It was a soft, familiar voice. One that played through his dreams lately.

He was out the door in a flash.

* * * *

Amy pushed the still damp hair out of her face and wished she was seeing his condo under better circumstances. "I'm all right. You could have taken me home."

The elevator doors opened but not to some hallway. They were suddenly in his home and it was spectacular. She hadn't realized he was a man of quite these means.

She had a very lovely apartment close to her sister's building, but she'd had to downsize. She'd put a lot of her money back into Slaten, trying to buy up stock so she had a firmer hold on her own damn company.

Fighting the board was beginning to make her weary. They all wanted something from her. Most of all they wanted to tell her how much better things had been when her father had been in charge.

They didn't give a crap that he'd been ready to sell them all out. They only knew they weren't making as much cash as they had when her father had been there cheating every employee and cooking the books.

Flynn held the elevator door open for her. "You were in an accident. You need someone to watch you."

The ER doctor had been overly protective. Very likely because her sister was married to the head of Neurosurgery. "I had every test known to man run on me. They all came back fine. It was a little fender bender. Nothing more."

"Not according to the cops. That asshole hit you from behind and you ended up in the oncoming lane. You could have died."

"Well, that dumbass was texting his girlfriend, not trying to kill me. I'm fine." It had been a hell of a horrible day. She'd been sitting there minding her own business and waiting for the light to turn green when teenaged nitwit had rear-ended her so hard she'd drifted into the oncoming lane. "You're really doing far too much. I called because my cell was wrecked and unfortunately the police officer didn't know my sister's number."

When he'd asked she'd realized she relied far too much on speed dial. She'd looked down at the phone and there had been no Bridget page.

She couldn't remember her own sister's cell but she'd known Flynn's. She'd stared at his stupid number on her phone after he'd given it to her and somehow it had imprinted on her brain. He'd been the only number she could remember. She'd felt so dumb when she'd called him, but he'd been a trooper.

His eyes narrowed as he led her inside. "Yes, we'll have a talk about that in the morning."

"Talk about what? Oh, is this a Dom thing? You're using your Dom voice on me." It was a deep, rich voice that he only seemed to find when they were at the club or when she made the mistake of opening her own car door. That was a no-no for Flynn.

"Yes, it's a Dom thing. We have a contract. Do you remember what that contract states very plainly?"

She searched her memory. They'd gone over contracts on the first night and then the second class, she and Flynn had negotiated one of their own. It had been super fun. Just watching the man try to figure out how to ask about water sports had been more than enough reason to do the entire class. He'd seemed relieved that she wasn't into getting peed on as an aphrodisiac. She'd thought about drawing it out but decided it would be best to be honest. So what was he upset about tonight?

He'd been a perfect gentleman. He'd shown up at the ER and taken care of absolutely everything. He'd talked to her sister—after calling around and figuring out what her number was. Then he'd dealt with her brother-in-law, who had shown up in scrubs and intimidated all his ER peeps. Will had called Flynn out to the hallway where they'd seemed to have some Dom to Dom discussion about her care that had ended up with her here.

At least now she understood how Flynn was connected to Sanctum. He was Mitch Bradford's half brother. Mitch had been the lawyer who made sure the vote on the night of her wedding had been by the books. He'd been so different from Flynn. When Flynn wasn't a jealous ass, he was ridiculously sweet and attentive.

Now, though, he looked very stern. Unfortunately, it looked damn fine on him. He was all dominant and masculine. Very authoritative. He would make a stern teacher to play schoolgirl with.

Mr. Flynn, I seem to have forgotten my homework. And my underwear.

"Yes, it's a Dom thing. Our contract states plainly that you are to call me if you find yourself in need or in trouble. You are to ensure that you're out of danger. If you need to call the police, you can do that first, but after the immediate threat is over, I'm the first person you contact."

"I thought that was if I was like being stalked or got mugged or something. The text dude wasn't threatening after the accident. I think he peed his pants a little."

There were times when it was obvious he didn't find her sarcasm charming. "You could have been killed. So we're going to have a serious discussion about that infraction, but not tonight. Tonight, you're going to go and take a shower and I'm going to order Chinese food, and then we're going to sit on the couch and watch TV and I'm going to calm down. Stay here and I'll get things started for you."

He stalked toward the back of the condo.

He might be more upset than she was. She'd been scared when she'd realized she was out of control, but then she'd been okay. She'd talked to the driver of the other vehicle and made sure everything was all right with him. She'd done what she normally did. She'd taken control of the situation in a calm and reasonable fashion.

Flynn had shown up and taken care of her when she'd been hurting and scared. He'd rushed into her ER room and he'd taken her hand in his and she'd known she could relax.

It had been a rough week, but when she'd needed him, he'd been there.

Maybe it was time to reassess their situation. Since the first night he'd shown absolutely no signs of being a nasty prick. Had he been honest with her? Had she thrown him off balance?

The truth was she had so little time with him when she thought about it. The class lasted six weeks and they were done with one of them. If he hadn't been such a jerk that first night she probably would already be sleeping with him.

What had he been through? Who'd hurt him? He was in his thirties so it was likely that someone along the way had broken his heart. They'd kept things casual during their meetings.

Dates. They were a lot like dates. Not the classes, but afterward he would take her to dinner and he always paid even when she offered. He would give her that look and she would find her hand moving away from the check. He picked her up before class—that was in their contract—and made sure to walk her to her door after dinner.

He walked back in, looking deliciously yummy in his slacks and open-throated shirt that showed off tan skin. She happened to know that smooth skin covered a lot of muscle.

Outside, the rain made the lights of Dallas look hazy and a bit surreal.

She wanted to feel good. It had been so long. Was it wrong to ask him if he wanted to feel good, too?

He stopped in front of her, his face softening. "Are you all right? Will told me I should call him if you started to feel pain."

The accident had been minor. She hadn't even taken an aspirin.

But she'd been scared as she'd gone into the oncoming lane and seen a truck coming her way. She'd realized that it sucked to be dying when she hadn't even lived. She'd spent her whole life trying to please a father who couldn't love her, living in the shadow of her larger than life rebellious sister, being dutiful, and what had it gotten her? She wasn't happy. She'd taken over Slaten, but that had been about duty, too.

Couldn't she have one thing that was just for her? It wouldn't last forever, but for a while she could feel free.

"I feel fine." That wasn't being honest. "My body is fine, Flynn."

He moved into her space but somehow his height, his overwhelming presence, didn't intimidate her. It comforted her. "And the rest of you? Sweetheart, you're crying."

She had to chuckle at that. "I don't do that around anyone but you, damn it."

His big hand came up and cupped her cheek, thumb swiping away the tear. "I don't want you to hide things from me."

"What are we doing, Flynn? I know why we're both in the class, but not everyone goes out afterward. Are we dating? It's okay if we're not. If we're just getting to know each other so we can get through the class, that's okay."

He stared at her for a moment as though trying to figure out what to say. And then he moved in again, their bodies almost touching. "I've been trying to get to know you."

"Because I'm your partner?"

"Because you're the first woman to move me in a very long time and I want to know if that's real or something I made up in my head because I'm lonely." His hand found her hair, smoothing it back.

She was sure she resembled a drowned rat, but he was looking at her like she was something lovely. There was nothing he could have said that would have moved her more. He could have talked dirty or told her in sweet terms how much he wanted her. He could have told her he wanted to see where it went.

He was lonely. She was so fucking lonely, and somehow when he was close to her she didn't feel it.

"Then I must have made it up, too," she admitted. "I like being around you, Flynn. I don't think about how shitty my life is when I'm around you."

His gaze threatened to melt her. "What are you asking me for,

Amy? Are you asking me to play? I can do that. Anything sexual between us is likely going to include D/s. Or I can simply take care of you. I started a shower. It should be warm by now. I can let you go and get cleaned up and I'll be the perfect gentleman."

She didn't need a gentleman tonight. "Or you could be my Dom."

"Your Dom is going to want more than to rub your feet. I don't want to take advantage of you. You've had a rough day."

"And playing would make it so much better, Sir. Please kiss me. Please make this shitty day have something good happen in it. I'm not asking for a collar. I want to spend the next couple of weeks exploring this with you. Maybe it works out. Maybe it doesn't. We can still be friends if we make the choice at the beginning that if it doesn't happen for us, that's how we'll end it. Hell, maybe we'll find out we're not sexually compatible."

"Not possible," he said, his lips looming over hers. "Let me off the leash, Amy. Tell me we're playing. Our contract allows all manner of sexual play. Let me take control."

All she wanted was for this man to kiss her. She'd kissed him the first time. She'd been in control and it had felt magical. What would it feel like when he was the one kissing her? Would he be dominating or soft and tender?

A thrill went through her system. The last time she'd been kissed it had come out of nowhere from a coworker. The sex that had followed after a couple of dates had been nice, but she hadn't had this wild anticipation, her heart pounding, blood heating. She'd never wanted a man the way she wanted Flynn. She'd cared about a few men. She'd wanted sex before. But now it was all mashed up in an incredible need that she was pretty sure only he could fill.

She'd never been dominated by a man before. She typically took charge when it came to sex. She wasn't sure if it was because she'd mostly found her partners at work and she'd been the boss's daughter and then the boss. The first time she'd truly felt a spark for a man had been Frankie, who was wildly dominant.

What would it be like with a man who wanted her sexually? And yes, who she was really starting to like. She'd desired him the minute she'd seen him, but after a few dates, she was rapidly falling for the man.

Her skin tingled as she looked up into his handsome face. His jawline was perfectly straight and there was the slightest hint of a five-o'clock shadow.

"Yes, Flynn. Play with me. Take control."

His mouth came down on hers. Pure heat flooded her system. Flynn didn't seem to care that her hair was still damp. His hand fisted in it, drawing her head back to give himself better access. His lips moved over hers in an expert fashion. The man knew how to kiss. His tongue came out, dragging along her lower lip and tempting her to open for him.

She relaxed against him, allowing his tongue inside to play with hers. She let her hands find his waist. He was lean and muscular, and she was reminded of how long it had been since she'd been held by a man who wasn't trying to comfort her.

This wasn't about comfort at all. His mouth seduced her, tempted her. The hand in her hair tightened slightly. A flare of pain lit up her scalp and she could feel her nipples hardening to peaks. She couldn't help herself. She moved against him, needing to press herself to his warmth.

His hand left her hair and slid down to her backside, cupping her and hauling her against his body. She could feel exactly how much he wanted to play. His cock was hard. She couldn't resist rubbing her hips against him.

He hissed and stepped back. "Go take a shower, Amy."

"What?" His words didn't quite make sense.

"I said go take a shower. It should be hot by now. Don't argue with me. You gave me control. You have a safe word we agreed on that first night. Either do as I ask or we'll be done playing for the night. I'm not going to fuck you over the sofa after you've been in an accident. If you don't give me a minute to calm down, that's exactly what I'll do and I'll regret it. So go."

She wasn't so sure she would regret it, but he seemed determined to treat her like an invalid. He was being a gentleman when she so wanted him to be a nasty boy. Still, he'd explained. According to their contract he didn't have to do that while they were playing. He was already bending for her, so she nodded and moved away from him.

"It's in the back, through my bedroom," he explained.

Well, it hadn't been everything she'd hoped for, but that kiss had proven they were incendiary.

And that if she was going to get through the night, she needed some relief. She walked through the bedroom, not really seeing it. All she could think about was Flynn's hands on her. The shower was running, steam coming out of what looked to be a truly spectacular bathroom. There was a massive tub that had probably been built for three and a shower that was big enough to have an orgy in. She shucked her clothes and stepped into the shower with one thought only—finding some relief.

She moved under the rainfall showerhead and sighed. Naturally he'd gotten it to the perfect temperature. Everything the man did with the exception of that first night was perfect. He even had the perfect excuse to not sleep with her tonight. She couldn't complain since he was trying to ensure her comfort.

She would rather have him. He would be the perfect comfort after a shitty, shitty day.

He was likely out there right now calling in an order for Kung Pao chicken. They would sit in front of that god-awful enormous television of his and when he was certain she wasn't going to die on him, he would drive her home.

Damn, but she wished he hadn't changed his mind. She let her hand drift down, pretending it was his. His hands had been big and callused and they'd felt so right on her skin.

She could imagine them cupping her breasts, his thumbs flicking over her nipples. He would put his mouth there eventually, but the man seemed to like to take his time.

Not that she had much of it. He would probably think she'd slipped in the shower if she wasn't fairly quick.

She let her hand slide down to her clit. She needed this. She needed him, but he'd changed his mind so this would have to do.

It wasn't like she hadn't handled herself before. This was how she'd dealt with sexual frustration since her marriage. There hadn't been time for dating after the divorce so it had been her and her happy right hand.

She envisioned that it was Flynn's hand running over her clitoris down to her pussy. It was his hand getting her hot and wet.

"What the hell do you think you're doing?"

She screamed and nearly slipped. She would have fallen had Flynn not been there to catch her. In his very naked arms. Which went with the rest of his naked, muscular body.

Holy hell.

He lifted her up with ease and set her back on her feet. His dark eyes were staring down at her. They held her for a moment but then she couldn't help but look at him. Because he was really there. So there. Beautifully, gorgeously there.

He had a big dick. It was hard and damn near reached his navel, which was attached to some spectacularly defined abs. Washboard abs. She'd heard the term, seen them on TV. God, that guy in *Dart* had gorgeous abs, but this was the first time she'd seen washboard abs up close and personal.

She kind of wanted to lick them.

"I asked you a question, Amy. I expect an answer. Eyes up here."

She was fairly certain her whole body went a nice shade of pink. "I thought we were done playing. You're naked."

Smart. That was smart, Captain Obvious. His shoulders were so broad. She'd thought they'd looked broad in his shirt. They were even broader without clothes. He shouldn't ever wear clothes. He looked so yummy without them.

His hand came out, tilting her chin back up because her eyes seemed determined to roam his body. "I thought it was best since we were going to take a shower. I can see that you've made the wise decision to shower undressed as well. However, I think you're about to find that deciding to masturbate was an unwise choice."

She winced. He'd caught her masturbating. Shouldn't she be way more embarrassed about that than she was? Seeing him naked had thrown her off her shame game. "I thought you were done. I thought you were sending me away and we were through playing."

He shoved a hand through his hair, slicking it back. It reached the top of his shoulders and made him look a little savage. Yeah, that was hot, too. "I never said that. I said I needed a moment. I took it. I called in our dinner and it's an hour away. That's more than enough time for me to get you cleaned up and comfortable, and the play will last until I drop you off at work in the morning. It will begin again when I pick you up tomorrow afternoon. We'll have dinner and then go to class and it will continue until such time as your car is replaced and I'm satisfied you're all right. Do I make myself clear?"

She'd wondered how she would get to work in the morning. She'd been planning on calling in a rental. It looked like she wouldn't have that expense. "Yes."

A single brow rose over his eyes. "Yes?"

"Yes, Sir." It was funny how she suddenly felt energized again.

"Did you not read the portion of your contract that stated when we're playing you're not allowed to masturbate unless I specifically ask you to? I seem to remember you had a name for that clause so I think you should recall it."

Yep. She'd called it the anti-rubbing-one-out rule. "I thought the play was over."

"It isn't over until I say it's over or you use your safe word. Now turn around and place your palms on the bench. I want your feet about shoulder width apart."

"What?" He was kidding, right? He didn't look like he was kidding. He looked twelve kinds of serious.

"Do it now, Amy. I'm planning nothing more right now than a warm-up spanking and for it to serve as a reminder, but if you say another word, it's going to be a real punishment."

He wanted to spank her. She'd thought a whole lot about that spanking. She'd played at it. Role-play was something she'd always loved, and she'd run through some scenarios with past boyfriends. She'd had her ass spanked by a couple of them and she'd enjoyed it. Somehow she thought this would be different from the light, playful smacks she'd had before.

Flynn would be serious about it.

Without another thought, she turned and put her hands flat on the tiled bench. Her backside was totally on display.

"You said you wanted to explore your sexuality, Amy. Is that still true?"

She'd told him that the first night when he'd asked why she was taking the class. "Yes, Sir."

"Even if it means exploring it with me and me alone because for the duration of this class, if we're involved in a sexual relationship, I want to be the only man. That's a hard limit for me. You need to understand that."

She didn't understand it. Not entirely, but she'd begun to suspect that he'd been hurt in the past. Not that everyone hadn't on some level. She kind of thought he'd probably been cheated on. It would explain some of his reaction in the beginning. The good news was she didn't want to see anyone but him. "I'm fine with that, Sir. I would like to explore together and see where it goes."

No real strings. No expectations beyond getting to know one another and having a very nice time. They could relax and know things were somewhat settled for the next month. No sitting around and wondering what was happening or if he would call. He would because they had a contract.

"Then we should begin as we mean to go," Flynn said. "No masturbating while we're playing."

The sound rattled her. It was a loud *SMACK* and then pain flared across her ass. Hot and fast, he kept it up, his big palm raining fire on her skin.

Tears pierced her eyes and she bit back a groan. The pain sank into her. Those playful taps she'd taken before had nothing on what Flynn was doing to her. She'd giggled through those but this overwhelmed her.

After ten or twelve, he stopped, his hand still on her cheek. "That clit only gets stroked by me. I would like you to acknowledge that."

"Yes." She just wanted him to touch her again. Somehow he knew exactly how to spank her. When he touched her she practically felt sparks between them. Even now her skin was hot and aching for more. It was pleasure and pain all wrapped up in something that made it more than either experience was singularly. The pleasure was heightened by the pain.

A crack split the air. "Use your words, pet."

He apparently liked to hear her talk dirty. She could give him that. "My clitoris belongs to you. Only you can touch it, stroke it. Only you can make me come."

For as long as it lasted, they would play, and part of that play was surrendering control to him and that included her pleasure.

It was an intoxicating idea. Every day she slogged through, having to make decision after decision. Being in charge of everything, responsible for everything, was tiring. She wouldn't give up her job for anything in the world, but she needed this. She needed these hours when she had to worry about nothing but pleasing him. When the world narrowed down to something manageable and she knew she could focus on what brought her pleasure.

She was fairly certain he would bring her an enormous amount of pleasure.

He spanked her again, slower this time so she felt every single second. A hard smack would be followed by the hot feel of his hand cupping her, holding the heat to her. He struck the under curve of her ass, making her feel needy. She could feel herself softening, getting ripe and ready.

"You're beautiful, pet. I knew you would look lovely, but this ass is quite perfect."

She bit her bottom lip to keep from crying out. Now that she was here she realized how on the edge she was. She'd held it together through the accident. Not once during the police questioning or the ride to the hospital had she been anything but collected and patient.

Flynn was sending her somewhere else. He slapped her ass with that big hand of his and she couldn't be rational about it. The pain made her eyes water, and somehow crying made her look inward. It took her back to that moment when she'd realized the car was out of control and that no one needed her. Not really. Bridget had a family. Frankie would find his perfect lover and be happy. No one would miss her. They would install another CEO and life would go on. No one would mourn her with their whole hearts.

She found herself hauled up, strong arms coming around her. Flynn balanced her, surrounded her. His arms wound under her breasts and held her tight, her back to his front.

"Tell me," he whispered in her ear.

"I was so scared."

"Of course you were." His voice was soft against her. "You could have been killed. Don't hold it in. You don't have to do that. Let it out. You're safe now. Let it out."

Amy never let it out. That wasn't something they did in her family. Well, Bridget had done it. Bridget had been the rebel. Amy had been the good girl, the controlled one.

But Flynn was in control now. He wanted her to let go. He wouldn't judge her for it.

"I didn't want to die." A sob formed in the back of her throat.

"I know, pet."

She shook her head. "Not because my life is so great. I didn't want to die because no one would miss me."

His arms tightened again, a sweet cage. "You are so wrong, but don't stop. Let it out. Let it all out."

She cried for the first time in forever. The pain had made it possible, as though it had been all right to cry over a physical ache, and then Flynn had given her permission to cry over the ache in her soul. She knew that wasn't right. It was a leftover from her crappy childhood when her father wouldn't tolerate normal emotions. They were a weakness and he didn't like weakness.

She hadn't even cried with Frankie, who she'd loved. He wouldn't have minded. God, she hadn't even cried after she'd signed the divorce papers. She'd loved him but she'd always known it was futile. Like her life. Wasted and impossible and useless.

It came at her like a tidal wave, and she found herself turned in his arms and crying against his chest. She clutched at him, needing to be so close. Somehow in the warm intimacy of the shower what had started as something sexual had become so much more intimate. No one in the world had seen her like this. Stripped and raw. No one had seen her because she'd been convinced no one could want her like this.

Flynn's hand moved on her hair, soothing down her back and up again. She could feel his cock hard against her belly, but he wasn't going to use it. He wouldn't. Not until the time was right. He would give her this tenderness, this affection she hadn't realized she needed so very badly.

"You're all right, pet. You're okay here with me." He kissed her forehead. "I was scared, too. When you called. I was more scared than I probably should be. I don't know what's going on between us, but I don't want to lose you now. Tell me you're real."

She looked up at him, unsure of what he meant. She was sure she looked real to him now. There was no way her face wasn't puffy, her nose red. "I'm very real, Flynn."

Something passed over his face, some unnamed emotion, and then he leaned over and kissed her, his lips sweet on her own. "I would have missed you, Amy. I want to be the first person you call. Now tell me how you feel."

Lighter than before. Her chest was still hitching from leftover emotion, but she felt happier than she had in a very long time. "I'm good, Sir."

He turned her again and there was that monster cock, nestling against the small of her back. "Let me make you feel even better."

His hands slid over her breasts. There was still a hard ache in her backside she would likely feel in the morning. It didn't stop her from wiggling against him, trying to feel him. He caught her nipples and gave them a hard tweak.

"Stop. This is my time. I want to be the reason you fall asleep tonight and wake up happy and rested in the morning. Let me take care of you. There'll be plenty of time for fast and hard later. Tonight you take only what I give you."

She sighed. He was going to be a hard-ass about this and he'd already given her so much. She couldn't refuse him now. "Yes, Sir."

His left arm snaked around her chest, held her tight against him while his very clever right hand made its way down her torso. "Do you masturbate often?"

"Apparently not anymore."

Her nipple got another tweak that had her yelping. "Don't be a brat."

"I do it to relax. It's the only sex I've had in about eighteen months. Don't make me out to be some prude though, Flynn. I was married and then I…my job got complex." She didn't want to go into it with him.

"You didn't have sex while you were married?" The question was whispered against her ear, the heat of his mouth making everything seem so damn erotic.

How to answer that question without going in to work? Mitch wouldn't have talked to him about Slaten, but she knew what her family's reputation was like. She didn't want him to think poorly of her. Surely that could wait until later. "It was a marriage of convenience. He's a friend of mine and he needed a wife for business purposes. It's over now, but no, we didn't sleep together. It was simpler that way."

If they stayed together for any amount of time, he would meet Frankie and then she would have to deal with those explanations, but for now she wanted to revel in Flynn. She didn't want him in her everyday, crappy world. She wanted to hoard him like her secret stash of happiness. The minute he entered her world, he would be subject to her family's awfulness.

"You're getting tense again." He nipped at her earlobe. "I'm going to have to do something about that. You see, I'm not opposed to this little button getting pushed. I just want to be the one doing the pushing."

His finger slid over her clit and she sighed against him, her body arching into his touch.

"Relax." The words were whispered, but she knew an order when she heard one. There was a deep command in his voice even when it was quiet. "Let me take care of you."

The words themselves were pure seduction. Take care of her. No one took care of her. She'd been taught to take care of herself, to not trust anyone. To be reliant on someone was weakness and weakness should be ruthlessly purged.

But that was her father's world. She didn't have to live in that world. Not here. Not now. This was why she'd chosen to take the class in the first place. So she could find another world. In Flynn's world she didn't have to be strong every minute of the day. She didn't have to be in control. He wanted the responsibility, craved and needed it. They were giving each other something. She wasn't simply taking.

She let her head roll toward his neck. He was so tall. Taller than her. So often she was the tallest woman in the room, but Flynn made her feel delicate and petite. His hand moved in perfect rhythm.

"What do you think about when you touch yourself?"

"Lately I think about you."

"I want to be the only one you ever think about," he whispered as his finger pressed down and rotated in a circle. "Let yourself go."

The orgasm rushed over her, hitting her hard and making her shake in his arms.

He held her as she came down from the high. He held her as

tenderly as he'd held her when she cried. After a moment, he turned her, the sweetest smile on his face.

"Now let's get you cleaned up and ready for dinner."

She looked down. His cock was still hard as a rock.

"Should I take care of you?" Her whole body felt like a limp noodle. Happy. Sated.

He reached out for the shampoo. Thank god the man had a full lush head of hair and looked like he knew how to take care of it. He actually had conditioner. "There's time enough for that. Like I said. This is my time. I want to take care of you."

As he soaped up her hair, she realized how nice it was to be John Flynn's sub.

It was something she could definitely get used to.

Chapter Four

Flynn sat back, the arousal he felt oddly comforting. It was anticipation. It was the satisfaction he felt when he knew he'd done something really well.

Amy was practically asleep in his arms. When he'd shown up at the hospital, she'd been a ball of nerves. Oh, she'd tried to cover it up with polite smiles and that very reasonable tone of hers, but he'd seen past it. When Amy smiled, she lit up the fucking world. He wasn't sure who he'd been watching in that ER, but it wasn't his sub. His sub was vibrant and alive and something had shut her down.

Like he'd shut her down that first night.

He'd been worried it had been the accident, that she'd been in pain. He'd quickly come to realize that this was the Amy the rest of the world got to see. This was work Amy.

He'd managed to get her back to the Amy he'd come to know. She was smiling and making jokes about the Kung Pao chicken and cuddling up against him like he was her teddy bear while they watched TV.

It was so worth the freaking hard-on he'd had for two hours. It was making him the slightest bit dizzy. Probably from all the blood in his dick.

"I love it when he takes out three people with one dart," she murmured before sighing and letting her head rest down on his shoulder.

Once he'd dried her off and gotten some food in her, she'd become a happy little kitten.

God, he felt fucking good. Having her cry in his arms, having her trust him, it was the ultimate high.

Now they were sitting on his sofa and watching her favorite show with her favorite actor. He kind of wanted to punch Jared Johns in his perfect abs. He'd never realized how often the dude shed his shirt. He was supposed to be a superhero with a secret identity, but the man liked going shirtless. He'd also noticed how much each episode was devoted to his workouts.

"You get enough to eat?" He liked the peace he found sitting beside her.

"It was good. Yes, thank you, Sir." She yawned. "Were you serious about me staying over tonight?"

There was zero way he was taking her home. Not now that he had her here. Not now that he'd touched her and held her and knew how sweet she looked when she came. He was going to keep her beside him as long as he possibly could.

Maybe then he could figure out exactly what she was doing.

He wanted to believe her. God, he wanted to tell her everything right fucking now and get this all out in the open, but she hadn't told him the truth. He'd asked about her job and she'd deflected. He still needed more time, but he was starting to suspect that whatever was going on with Amy, he wouldn't give her up no matter what.

If she was playing him, he would punish her, but that didn't mean he couldn't keep her.

"I was serious. I don't suppose I could convince you to stay home with me tomorrow?"

She went still against him. "I'm all right."

"And if I just want you to stay?" If she was who she said she was, taking a sick day wasn't a big deal. Now the CEO of a company...that was a different story.

"I can't. I...I've used up all my sick days. I have to go in, but I would love to stay the night if it's not a bother."

Not the answer he wanted. Still, he tightened his arm around her. "Not a bother. I'm perfectly happy to have you stay here. I told you how this is going to work for a while. At least until you get your car back. Unless you have a backup car."

She laughed. "No. Don't be silly. I was going to rent a car."

"I would prefer to drive you."

"Okay."

He was either falling deeper into her web or she was getting closer to him. It didn't matter tonight. Tonight, all that mattered was she was here.

"So, how are you really feeling? Will told me I should give you something if your muscles start to ache." It was the only damn reason he hadn't attacked her in the shower. Sometimes it took a few hours for the pain to set in. He didn't want to give her more. He could wait.

Her hand went to his thigh as she moved slightly away from him so she could look at his face. "I feel great. I feel better than great. I am tired though. Long day. Maybe we should turn in." She frowned. "I don't have a toothbrush."

Oh, she of little faith. "I had one delivered along with the prescriptions Will called in for you if you need them. One's for pain and the other is an anti-inflammatory."

"I don't need them." She sat back and it was the first time since the shower that she hadn't been touching him. "Where do you want me to sleep?"

"You can take my bedroom." He probably wouldn't sleep at all. He would sit out here and work. It was what he usually did at night. He would sit in his perch high above the city and work until it was almost dawn. "The bed is very comfortable."

"But you won't be in it."

This was the moment he'd been waiting for, kind of dreading and desperately anticipating all at the same time. "Not if I think I could hurt you."

She huffed a little and stood up. "I'll be back."

He reached out and gripped her wrist. "Where do you think you're going?"

"To find a doctor who will write me a note so you'll have sex with me."

He couldn't help but smile at that. She was pouting like a kid who'd lost her favorite toy. This was why he'd pushed her to cry in the shower. He needed this Amy back. His Amy. He'd hated how polite and courteous she'd been when they'd been in public. Oh, she'd allowed him to handle some things, but her smile hadn't reached her eyes and not a single sarcastic remark had passed those luscious lips of hers. It was wrong and counter to everything he'd come to know about her.

This Amy boldly told him what she wanted and was willing to do whatever it took to get it.

This Amy wanted him.

"I think I can handle this without a note." He needed to make her understand. "I wasn't turning you down, pet. I was attempting to be a good Dom. If you're telling me you need comfort and affection more than you need rest, I will reevaluate my stance on our sleeping arrangements."

She stopped for a moment. "I feel fine. The ER trip was overkill. I'm going to feel so much worse if you don't want me."

One of the things he'd come to adore about her was the fact that she'd been crazy honest with him when it came to sex and what she wanted out of D/s.

At least it felt like honesty. Her desire and arousal and completion had felt so real to him. More real than anything he'd had in forever. He didn't want to think about the rest of it. He wanted to sink into her.

Wasn't all of this a fantasy anyway? Playing took them out of their real lives and into something else.

"I want you so badly I can barely breathe."

She frowned. "Then why won't you touch me?"

"I've touched you." He could still remember how soft she'd been against his fingers.

"Not the way I want."

"I told you, I was trying to be a good Dom. I want to be that for you." He meant it. He took the class seriously, the lifestyle seriously. He wanted to be a good Dom and that meant putting her needs first.

All of them. Except his real name and real employer. He'd been honest about his occupation. He truly was a software developer.

Guilt swamped him but he told himself he would tell her the truth once he'd settled on a plan. It was too early to give himself away.

She pulled his T-shirt over her head and he realized she hadn't been wearing any underwear. Yeah, he might have neglected that but she hadn't said a thing. She'd been sitting there for an hour with nothing but his old T-shirt covering that gorgeous body of hers. "I want to be a good sub. I want to please my Dom in more ways than simply obeying him. Flynn, I loved what happened between us in the shower. I can't tell you how much, but there was something missing because you didn't let me give back to you."

His whole body tightened and he reached over for the remote. On the big screen, Dart was saving his city, but there were more important matters to attend to and he didn't want her thinking about anyone but him. He flicked the TV off and then reached for the lamp.

He hadn't closed the shades so the lights of the city filtered in through the room.

She smiled and he could see the way her nipples had tightened. "Wow. That is quite a view. It's like we're out in the open."

"But we're not. The windows are coated. It would be hard to see inside even if a helicopter flew by." He liked the idea of taking her this way, with the night and the city all around them. He kind of liked the idea that someone out there could be watching them, seeing her and knowing she only belonged to him. "Have I told you how fucking gorgeous you are? Don't move. Just stand there for a moment. I didn't get the chance to properly look at you earlier."

He liked her like this, with her hair all wavy and a little out of control.

She smiled, but even in the low light he could see the way she blushed. "I need a flat iron. You had everything else I would use on my hair except that."

"You don't need it. You look stunning without it. You're always so carefully made up. Don't get me wrong. You're beautiful like that too, pet. But seeing you without makeup or your hair done is a revelation. Turn around for me." He sat back, enjoying the way the moonlight made her skin glow.

Her back was as lovely as her front, her hair touching her shoulder blades. "My hair isn't usually this long. I think it's a minor rebellion on my part. My parents firmly believed that I should always present myself as professionally as possible, and part of that was keeping my hair neat and fairly short. They also insisted on me playing field hockey at prep school because they thought it would keep me out of trouble and away from boys."

He had to grin at the thought. "Please tell me that led to some exotic experimentation."

Her head turned and he could see the glint of humor in her eyes. "There's nothing quite like a girls' field hockey team on the road with a hidden stash of vodka. I learned how to kiss on that trip."

Fuck, he loved how open she was. She wasn't telling him because she was trying to seduce him. She was telling him because she talked too much, as though everything spilled out of her because she'd waited too long to tell someone.

"My swim team did not have the same fun," he admitted. "But I'll have to thank whoever taught you how to kiss because she did a phenomenal job."

Even in the moonlight he could see the way she blushed. "God, I can't believe I told you that. I'm such a moron. It's not like we had a relationship or anything. We played around, I guess. We were all lonely girls."

He was going to put a stop to that. He stood and moved in, letting his hands find her shoulders, his lips the nape of her neck. Such soft skin. Warm and inviting. "Hush. I want to hear all your stories. Especially the ones that involve sexual experimentation. I wouldn't care if you'd had a girlfriend before. I won't care how many men you've been with or what kind of crazy shit you did in your youth. I only care that you're here with me now. I care that whatever experiences you had before made you the lovely woman you are today. So I'll thank the girl who taught you to kiss and whatever lovers taught you to ask for the things you want. Do you have any idea how sexy that is to me?"

"I like being able to speak my mind. It's hard where I work. A woman in my position is supposed to always be in control. I can't show anger or sorrow or anxiety. I definitely can't say what I want to say."

He slid his hands down her arms. "You can with me. There's nothing you can't tell me. I was an asshole that first night because I knew you were important. That's not who I really am. I'm not saying I won't be possessive, but I won't judge you, Amy. I want to play and relax and get to know the real you."

"Then let's play because I need it. I think I need it more than I could have imagined."

He felt the same way. Standing here in the quiet of the night with her naked and trusting made him feel ten feet tall. It made the rest of the world dissolve away. He didn't have to worry about Chase or the business or even what would happen later. There was only the here and now, and that meant having her in every way.

"I want you to undress me."

She turned and her hands immediately went to the bottom of his T-shirt. He'd put it on after the shower, along with boxers and a pair of sweats he'd hoped would hide the monster. They'd simply tented and showed off how aroused he was. That was all right now that they'd sorted through how the evening would go.

She dragged the shirt up and over his outstretched arms and then paused, staring at his chest.

Damn but that made him feel good. He didn't care if she watched the guy on TV as long as she looked at him like that.

"Touch me."

Her hand came up and she placed her palm on his chest and sighed, as though she reveled in the contact. One day he was going to have her hard and fast, but he gritted his teeth because today was not the one. Today she got to explore and he got to endure.

She ran her hands over his chest, her palms soft against his skin. Everywhere she touched him, his skin seemed to come to life. She took her time, very likely enjoying some revenge on him for everything he'd done in the shower with her. After he'd spanked her and made her come, he'd taken forever washing her hair and soaping her body.

He'd never spent so much time on a woman before. Sex had been good, but that single shower with Amy had been the most intimate experience of his life.

He wanted to continue it.

"Why haven't you been married, Flynn?" She asked the question as she walked around him, placing those sweet hands of hers on his back. "Or have you and you didn't mention it?"

Her hand ran down his spine and it took everything he had not to shiver. They were like butterflies running over his flesh. "I was engaged. It didn't work out."

"Oh. Can I kiss you? Your skin, I mean."

"Amy, touch me with anything you like, pet. It's very unlikely that

I'll ever tell you not to touch me. It would be very specific play and it would be about discipline, not because I don't want you."

He could feel her smile against his skin before she kissed his spine. "Not one of those cold, controlling Doms, are you?"

"Well, you're not exactly the type of sub who would respond to rigidity. I think they matched us quite well." If he put aside the fact that she owned a rival corporation, he would say they were perfectly matched. She needed attention and affection, and a routine that involved both. She needed someone who would take care of her when she wasn't having to take care of everything else.

He needed to be needed. He needed a woman who wanted him for something more than money and power, who put up with his quirks and shook him out of his single-minded focus on work.

Like she was doing now. He didn't want to think about anything but how good her lips felt on his back.

"I still talk to my ex. He's my friend. I hope that won't be a problem."

Her male model ex? "How close are you?"

"As close as a girl and her gay best friend can possibly be." She moved around again, looking up at him. "You did that very well, Sir. Not even a hint of violence."

It was so nice to be able to punish her when she was bratty. Even as he smiled, he reached out and tweaked her nipple with a nasty twist. He was perfectly satisfied when her eyes flared and her breath hitched. "Watch it, pet. I'm enjoying this play. I don't want to have to stop it for another spanking. And yes, I'm much happier knowing he's gay."

She gave him a brilliant smile. "I would like you to meet him. He's coming back in town in a few weeks. Maybe we can have dinner."

It was nice that she was thinking of their future. "Of course. Now take these off me. They've gotten far too tight."

Her eyes came up, wide and innocent even as she slipped her fingers under the waistband of his sweats. "So I shouldn't expect to have dinner with your ex?"

So she wanted to play it that way? "No. I haven't seen her in years and that's a good thing. Are you going to explore or should I kiss you and take you to the bedroom?"

He didn't want to talk about Jenna with her. It would lead to a discussion of his father and money and where he'd gotten his, and he didn't want that tonight. He wanted to forget about everything that might come between them and concentrate on what brought them together.

"I think I'll explore." She dropped to her knees, dragging the sweats down with her. She left him in nothing but his boxers. Her head came up, eyes finding his. "Have I told you how beautiful you are, Sir?"

No woman had ever told him that before. He'd been told he was hot. Sexy. Never beautiful. It was funny what a simple word could do to him. He put a hand on her hair. "No and thank you, pet. I very much appreciate the way you look at me."

An impish grin lit her face. "I've found the most beautiful men are also the most in need of affirmation." She pulled down his boxers and his cock sprang free. "Let me affirm that this is a gorgeous piece of male equipment."

It was definitely the neediest part of him. "Touch it."

"With pleasure, Sir. I do believe you said I could touch you anywhere I liked and with anything I liked." She leaned forward and suddenly her lips were on his cockhead. "I think I'll explore like this."

He damn near came when she ran her tongue over the head of his dick. Heat flashed through him like a lightning storm. His hands curled into fists because he wanted more than anything to reach for her hair and force her to take him deep.

Instead he watched her. She moved her hair to the side and he could see the way she rolled her tongue over him. She licked the stalk of his cock, from the head to right where the base met his balls. They felt heavy and drawn up, waiting to shoot off.

She took him in hand and stroked him while she ran her tongue over his weeping slit. She lapped up the arousal she found there and then sucked him behind her lips.

The heat of her mouth threatened to undo him. If he let her, she'd likely continue until he couldn't take it anymore and he came in her mouth.

He reached out and gently fisted a hand in her hair. "Not tonight, pet. Tonight I want more than a blow job. Come here."

She came up and into his arms with an eagerness that felt like joy.

It seemed to flow from her and into him as she lifted her lips for his kiss.

He took her mouth, hungry for more of what she could give him. He drew her body to his, loving the way her breasts nestled against his chest. She opened for him, inviting his tongue to play with hers. No hesitation. She knew what she wanted and it was him. It was a fucking heady experience. Amy didn't play around when it came to sex. She didn't pretend or prevaricate. She wanted to get him in bed, and damn but that seemed like the right thing to do.

He bent over and picked her up, lifting her high against his chest.

A little squeal came out of her mouth as though that had been the last move she'd expected. "You're going to throw out your back."

She cuddled close to him though.

"With you? Not on your life." She was delicate in his arms, and yet there was something solid about her form. She was slender but strong. "Hush and let me ravish you."

Her eyes lit up. "Like a Viking barbarian? And I'm a nun or something."

Oh, she had an imagination. "Absolutely not. You're definitely the prettiest lady in the village and not a nun. I'm a very traditional Viking."

He tossed her on the bed and went to the nightstand to get his very traditional condom. He was definitely going to need it.

"I think you would make a good Viking."

"I think this particular Viking is also a Dom." He wasn't going to let this get out of control. "Spread your legs for me."

She moved up, sitting up slightly so her back was against the pillows at the headboard. "Like this, Sir?"

She had to know what that breathy "Sir" did for him. She could likely see his dick jump every time she said it. Amy moved her long legs apart, bending them at the knees and giving him a glorious view of that pussy he'd already pleasured. It was ripe and glistening in the low light. She looked primal and wanton, as tempting as Eve must have looked to Adam. If Amy had been his Eve, he would have eaten that fucking apple, too.

He would settle for having a taste of something else.

He crawled across the bed, between her legs. Flynn breathed her in, the scent of her arousal so damn intoxicating.

He looked up her body and Amy was biting her bottom lip, her face flushed. She wanted this, wanted him.

It was all he needed.

He put his mouth on her and had his first taste. She was rich and he couldn't get enough of her. He let his tongue run over her clitoris and down through her labia. He speared her with his tongue, fucking deep while he spread her. He held her down even as she shook under him. He tongued her, drinking in her every pant and breathless whisper.

"Please, Flynn. Please."

Everything about this pleased him. Her taste. Her smell. The smooth feel of her skin, and definitely that desperate tone to her voice.

It was time to give her what she needed so he could find what he wanted more than his next breath. To be inside her.

He pressed a finger deep inside her, curling up. She was so tight, so hot. She would clench down on his dick.

He found her clitoris and licked her. He looked up her body. Her head was thrown back in complete ecstasy, her body bowing. She only needed a little more to push her over the edge.

He sucked her clit between his lips and was rewarded with her screaming out his name.

It was all he needed. He got to his knees and reached for the condom, rolling it on his cock. He was off the leash and let go of all that control he'd exercised. He didn't need it now. She could handle him. He got between her legs again, his cock finding its place as he pressed in.

She was so wet, but he still got a thrill from how tight she was, how her eyes widened as he forced his way in. Her hands came up and she clutched him.

So good. She felt so good around him. She surrounded him, his cock deep inside, her arms and legs winding around his body as though she was afraid to let him go.

He could have told her nothing would make him let her go.

He plunged in, thrusting his cock inside over and over. He could feel her nails digging into his flesh as she came again, but it didn't matter. It was one more sensation to be had.

He held it off as long as he could, but finally he felt his whole body tighten and the orgasm rushed through him. He pushed in as deeply as he could, not stopping until he'd given her everything he had.

He fell against her, letting the blood thrum through him in a pleasant rush. He breathed her in, the scent of their sex mixing with her shampoo. How long had it been since he'd been this intimate with a woman? He'd had sex, though lately not a lot.

This felt like something more. He'd signed a contract with her, to take care of her, protect her, see to her comfort. In exchange, he got this. He got her soft and sweet and submissive during sex.

It was a completely fair exchange.

He kissed her cheek. "I'll be right back."

She smiled up at him and sighed, settling down in the sheets. "I'll be here."

Flynn got up and made his way to the bathroom, taking care of the condom. He stretched, his body loose and relaxed. Fuck, but this was what he needed. He hadn't felt this good in forever.

He caught sight of himself in the mirror. Sure enough, she'd left little marks on his biceps where she'd held on to him.

He was lying to her.

Damn it. There it was. The guilt. It washed away the good stuff and he was left with the knowledge that they weren't settled. Not really. Either she was lying to him or he was lying to her. It was a wall between them and he didn't want it there.

So go back out there and talk to her. Settle it now. It's easy as pie. Get back into bed with her and talk about it there.

And if she walked out because her game was up, he would know it hadn't been real at all.

Anything was better than this terrible purgatory he found himself in. One minute he was in paradise, happy and sated, and the next there was a damn wall between them.

It was a wall he could tear down very quickly.

He strode back out, ready to have it out with her.

She was asleep, turned on her side, the moonlight making her look like an innocent goddess.

He slid in beside her and she rolled into his arms.

Tomorrow would be soon enough. He settled down and found himself falling asleep, dreaming of her.

* * * *

Amy looked around Flynn's kitchen, hoping he had some coffee. She never did well without a good jolt of caffeine.

Luckily, he had a lovely setup. It was a single cup coffee maker with a wide assortment of flavors. His whole condo looked to be meticulously kept. Like a five-star hotel.

Who the hell was her training Master?

She knew Mitch had money, but this was beyond what Mitch could afford. How was Mitch's brother so much more wealthy than he was? The condo itself had to be worth twenty million. It seemed awfully nice for a man who wrote code for a living.

She started the process that would bring her a hazelnut flavored coffee and looked around the kitchen.

Everything was top of the line and looked like it had never been used before.

It reminded her a little too much of the mansion where she'd grown up. There had been a staff dedicated to ensuring the place looked like a museum. If Amy had put down a cup, it was swiftly taken away even if she'd only had a sip. She'd never felt at home there. Not that it had been her home. It had been the place where she was shipped when school wasn't in session. Mostly for the summers. She could count the times she'd been allowed to go home for Thanksgiving and spring break on one hand.

But summers were different. Summers after she'd turned twelve had been about learning to work for Slaten Industries. Summers had been spent with the workers there, getting to know them, growing to care about them.

Was she going to fail them?

She thrust that thought out of her head. She was still in her Master's home. There was no place for it here.

Once the coffee was ready, she picked it up and held it in her hands, letting the aroma waft over her.

She was deliciously sore. And totally curious.

Flynn hadn't said much about his past beyond the fact that he had a couple of brothers and wasn't close to his parents.

Where had all this wealth come from?

She wandered to the living room and thought about slipping back into bed with him, but the clock told the tale. She needed to be in the office in an hour and that man liked to take his time. She hadn't had the heart to wake him. He'd been wrapped around her and she'd spent long moments studying his face in the early morning light.

He was beautiful and yet masculine at the same time. Lovely and still somewhat fierce.

She stood in front of the floor-to-ceiling glass windows and stared out at the slightly foggy Dallas morning. The city was starting to come to life around her.

She never did this, never stood and watched the sunrise. Perhaps that was because her view was of a parking lot.

The truth of the matter was she'd put everything she had in buying as much of her own stock as she could. Moving the corporate offices to Dallas had been expensive and she'd had to fight the board to do it. She'd thought at the time that it would be a new beginning, a way to get far from her father and his machinations.

She'd been wrong. He'd simply followed her and sat buzzing in the ears of her board members, whispering about how they'd made more money when he was the head, how she'd screwed everything up and profits were down.

Profits were down because Glendale kept stealing their clients. Yes, the move had been costly, but it would more than pay for itself in what they gained from lower taxes and the incentives the city had given them.

She just needed time. In two years, she would have Slaten back on top. It was all in her plan. All she needed to do was survive two years and she would be in a position where no one would question her place as CEO.

Time. She grimaced. She wasn't going to be on time for work today. Not unless she was willing to wake her sleeping lover and she wasn't. He'd been so kind to her, taking care of her, making love to her. She didn't want to repay that kindness by forcing him to conform to her insanely early hours. Most mornings she went into the office before the sun was up. There was no one there with the exception of the security officer, but by now her assistant would be on her way. She likely would worry if Amy wasn't already there, sitting at her desk.

She should get dressed and call a cab, but she didn't want the morning to end. Surely being an hour or two late once in her damn life wouldn't kill her. Staying in and fixing her Master some breakfast seemed like the proper way to repay him for all the care he'd shown her.

Maybe they could take another shower together before he took her back to her place and she had to get ready for the day.

But her assistant would worry and that could get the office gossiping. The last thing she needed was a rumor that she was sick or slacking off. She needed to explain to Val that she would be a few hours late and to deflect everyone by saying she had to deal with her car issues.

Except she also had phone issues. Like she no longer had a working one. Damn.

She turned and looked for a landline. She did know the number to get to Val's desk.

So why hadn't she called Val last night when she couldn't remember Bridget's number? That would have been the smart play. Val would have immediately called her sister and then Will would have shown up to take care of things. Instead, she hadn't even had a single thought of calling the office. She'd immediately turned to a man she'd only known for a week, as though she'd been waiting for something to happen so she could throw herself in his arms like one of Bridget's heroines.

She wandered back into the kitchen. No landline there. It looked like Flynn had joined the cellular revolution. If he had a landline it was for his Internet or security reasons. She had zero idea where his cell phone was.

But he had two computers sitting on a desk in what looked like his office space. The condo had a wide open floor plan, with only the kitchen, bedrooms, and bathrooms clearly delineated. The rest of the space was one large great room. In the back, close to the windows, there was a modern-looking desk with not one but two computers sitting on top. One was a laptop and the other a desktop. Both were plugged into massive screens.

Amy set her coffee mug down and approached the desk. Val read all her e-mail, even ones from strange addresses. She would send her assistant a quick note and then take the morning off. She'd seen some eggs in the fridge. She would poke around and try to find some toast or something to make pancakes out of. Then when she'd fed him, she could try to seduce him again. By the time she had to deal with her job, she would be relaxed and happy.

She sat down at his desk, in his big comfy chair. This was where he worked. She could picture him here, his hair tied back and eyes serious on the computer screen.

Excuse me, Mr. Flynn. You called for me?

Yes, I did, Amy. As my assistant, it's your job to always ensure that the boss is satisfied. Your work earlier today wasn't satisfactory. Those files were out of order. I'm going to have to spank you. Turn around and pull down your panties and then we'll talk about your job performance.

Yes, she could see that whole scenario playing out right here. He would spank her and make her get on her knees and suck his cock and then, oh, then he would lift her up and make her ride him right on this chair.

Maybe she would wake him up. With sex. That was a nice way to wake up. Maybe she would crawl back in bed with him and cuddle up, and when he finally woke, she would be right there, willing and ready to take care of her Master's every desire.

But not until she'd informed Val that she wasn't coming in. She touched the keys on the keyboard in front of her. It was attached to the mega tower that sat on the floor. She didn't know a ton about computers themselves even though she worked for a company that supplied services directly targeting computer and information systems. Her degree was in management. She had lovely IT guys to handle the technical end of things, and her job was to give them the best work environment, benefits, and pay she possibly could.

But she did know that Flynn's system was way more complex than her own. It looked like that sucker was attached to various hard drives. It was odd since most people would use thumb drives to back up, or the mysterious Cloud.

Flynn was old school. She liked it.

The screen came up but there was no screensaver. Just a flat black background and a request for a password. Even the font looked a little intimidating.

So she wouldn't be using this computer to e-mail.

"Would you like to tell me what you're doing?"

She damn near fell out of her seat. Amy gasped and then laughed a little as she saw Flynn standing in the hallway wearing nothing but his sweatpants. The man was way too yummy, but he'd scared her half to death. "Sorry. I wasn't expecting that."

"No, I suppose you weren't."

That was when she realized how narrow his eyes were, how his muscles seemed rigid.

She stood up. Apparently the man didn't like anyone sitting at his desk. "I'm sorry. I was trying to e-mail work. I thought I would go in a little late. I don't have my phone and I couldn't find a landline to call from so I decided to e-mail."

"I thought you couldn't possibly miss work. That's what you said last night." His voice was arctic cold.

She nearly shivered at the way he was looking at her. There was no happy lover in his gaze this morning. "A few hours won't hurt. I'm sorry. I should have asked you if I could use your system. I didn't think it would be a big deal."

He stared for a moment and she wished she was wearing more than his thin T-shirt. She felt exposed and she hated that.

"You should get dressed. I'll take you to your place and then to work," he said with finality.

"I thought we could have breakfast."

"I don't eat breakfast," he replied. "But I'll stop somewhere along the way if you need to. I have an early meeting. We should get going."

She hated how vulnerable she felt, but he was important. A choice was laid out in front of her. She could do what he asked and protect herself or she could try to figure him out. "What did I do?"

His jaw tightened and then he took a deep breath, as though forcing himself to relax. "I have sensitive material on that system. I don't let other people use it. You wouldn't have been able to send an e-mail out. It's not connected to the Internet."

She wasn't sure if she should try to hug him or go and get dressed. He seemed slightly softer than he had before, but he'd been so cold for a second. "I didn't know that. I don't know a lot about computers. I can type on one and use the software, but I'm crappy at fixing them. I assume everyone has Wi-Fi. Obviously I won't bother it again. I'll get a new phone today."

She had a lot more time now that she wouldn't be staying.

"Good. If there's anything I can do to help, let me know," he said, his voice turning excruciatingly polite. "There's a nice bakery next door to this building. Maybe we can grab a Danish for you."

She wasn't sure why, but he seemed to want to get rid of her. Maybe he didn't do the whole cuddly morning after thing. It hurt. It was a real, honest to god kick in the gut, but it wasn't like she'd asked him for a ring or anything. She'd gone into this casually, looking for some friendship with other women like her and the occasional nice night with a man like him.

So why had he given her so much more?

She gave him her brightest smile, the one she plastered on her face when she dealt with her board or difficult clients. Women in business didn't get to show their anger or their misery. It was always about the smile. "I'm fine. I'll grab a protein bar at my place. I should head in to the office. And I'll grab a cab. It's not a big deal. I'm going to get dressed. Thanks for last night. It was wonderful."

Amy started to move past him, willing herself to keep that fucking smile on her face.

He reached out and grabbed her arm. "I'm not used to people touching that system. In my business, someone is always out to steal the latest code."

Message received. Don't touch his shit. "Not a problem. Like I said, I'll have my phone back in a few hours. I promise, I know where the line is now. It was an innocent mistake and I wish you would stop looking at me like I tried to commit some sort of crime. I was trying to send an e-mail, Flynn. That's all."

"I've been burned before," he replied quietly. "Several times."

She softened slightly. She did understand corporate spying. Her father had practically been the CIA. It was why she hadn't gone after Glendale the way she should. She knew the sins her dad had committed against them. She didn't understand them entirely or why her father had hated Glendale in particular, but she knew the Adlers had been burned more than once by her father's deep belief in corporate espionage. "I'm sorry to hear that. I really wasn't trying to hurt you. I don't even know what you do. I don't have a reason to take something from you."

He stared down at her and for a moment she thought he was going to argue. Then he dragged her close and his mouth was on hers. He kissed her like a starving man, his tongue plunging deep.

He needed. She could feel it. She wasn't sure what it was he was asking her for, but she felt his bone-deep need. It poured off him, and everything that was soft and warm inside her responded. That affectionate part of herself bent to his will. She'd shoved it down for so very long. Her love and affection weren't needed in her father's world. It had been something to hide away and toss out because it had been useless.

Flynn needed it and she was determined to give it to him.

"Don't go," he said against her lips. "Stay with me."

It was all she'd wanted to do in the first place. "Yes."

He picked her up, hauling her high against his chest, but when she thought he would move back to the bedroom, he strode toward his desk. He sat down with her in his lap and flipped open his laptop. The screen was suddenly on, but she was thinking far more about the thick erection pressed against her backside.

"Type. Be fast. I don't want to wait," he growled against her ear.

He'd pulled up his e-mail and moved the cursor to where she would put in a name. His hands moved under her shirt, reaching up to cup her breasts as he licked and nipped at her ear.

How was she supposed to type when her whole body was busy responding to him? "Flynn, I'm going to make a mess of this."

"Type or I'll explain to your boss that you're far too busy pleasing your Master to come in to work today." He rolled her nipples, tweaking them enough to let her know he meant business.

That would go over so well. She quickly managed to type the words she needed to because her focus wasn't on that page. She clicked and it was sent.

"Good." He stood again, showing absolutely no sign of strain. "The rest of the morning is mine."

She held on and let her Master whisk her away.

Chapter Five

"I want you to run every test you possibly can on that machine." Flynn stared at the woman sitting at his desk, trying to let her know just how serious this was because she often didn't take a damn thing seriously with the exception of her own work. "Don't leave anything out. I want to know every single thing that was done to it."

Chelsea Weston frowned his way. "Would an ultrasound help? Do you think it got pregnant by another system? You know they get a little crazy during puberty."

She was brilliant but she could get sarcastic at times. Most of the time, really.

A chuckle came from the other side of the room. "Darling, you know Flynn has the equivalent of a chastity belt on that particular system. I scarcely think it's been unfaithful."

Of course her husband tended to indulge her.

Simon and Chelsea Weston owned the other half of the penthouse floor. They shared the outdoor space on the top of the building. He'd been surprised to find their half was kept in a lovely, peaceful garden where Chelsea did daily yoga. He'd heard rumors that Mrs. Weston had been seriously injured at one point, but he couldn't tell. Yes, she had some scars, but she was healthy and graceful, a fact she attributed often to her husband. They were an odd couple. He was a very British man who was rarely seen in anything but an impeccable suit. He'd heard stories from his brother that Weston had once been MI6, which meant he'd kind of been James Bond before he'd joined the McKay-Taggart team. Chelsea was Charlotte Taggart's sister and he was fairly certain she either worked for the CIA or some kind of government agency because some creepy dudes in black suits were always coming in and out of the building and they always visited her.

Still, they'd welcomed him and often asked him to join them for takeout at their place. He and Chelsea had bonded over their love of computers and their obsession with future tech. Their closest friends were Simon's partner, Jesse Murdoch and his wife, Phoebe, who also knew a thing or two about computers. When they all got together, he would find himself sitting with the women talking about tech while the guys grabbed a beer and discussed the best techniques for shooting the bad guys.

There were weeks when they were the only people he would spend any real time with.

He'd kind of hoped the next time he was invited, he could bring Amy with him so he wouldn't be the fifth wheel.

"If I thought an ultrasound would help me figure out what the hell happened this morning, I would call in a damn OB-GYN," Flynn admitted.

Weston sobered a bit, sitting back in the chair he'd taken and regarding Flynn seriously. "Why don't you tell me what happened?"

How to explain this without giving away too much? He trusted his friends, but he wasn't sure how close they were to Amy's side of the family. But this was one of the things Weston excelled at. He and Murdoch had worked plenty of corporate cases. "I told you how I've been dealing with some corporate espionage."

"You mentioned it."

Moment of truth. He was either going to find out how close he'd gotten to this couple or he would learn his place in the pecking order. It was a little sad that he was nervous about this. At one point in time he had plenty of friends. Now he was worried about losing the only ones he had. "My training partner is the CEO of the company that's been bombarding mine for years."

There was a feminine gasp from the office section of the room. "No way. Dude. That is the single most interesting thing I've heard in a very long time. Satan fucked up."

Weston frowned his wife's way. "Don't even start."

"Satan?" He had to ask.

Simon sighed. "Now she'll start. That is my sweet love's affectionate nickname for her brother-in-law. I do have to say I'm rather surprised that this didn't come up in the vetting process. They're usually quite thorough. Do you think it's Rycroft? Is he cutting corners?"

The last thing he wanted to do was get Wade in trouble. He was new and Flynn liked the big cowboy. "I can't imagine that he did."

"Kai and Wade don't run the background checks," Chelsea said, looking more animated than he'd ever seen her before. "That's a McKay-Taggart job. Ian makes the ultimate decision. He's the one who's cutting corners."

Weston stared at his wife. "Don't even think about it, love."

Chelsea flushed slightly, as though the deep voice had done something to her, but she soldiered on. "Can't you see that this is how we figure out what the hell he's doing? He's sending Li to parts of the world where we don't have ongoing jobs. He's been secretive and that crap he pulled letting the feds run a job in Sanctum a few months ago…that's not like Ian. This is how we get him to tell us what's happening."

Weston shook his head. "In the first place, *we* don't have ongoing jobs, love. You don't work for McKay-Taggart. You made that decision a very long time ago. Secondly, we're both going to stay out of it. When Ian needs us, he'll let us know."

"Even the Agency is blocking me," Chelsea said, her frustration evident in the tight line of her mouth.

Weston's eyes flared. "Excuse me? Are you forgetting we're not alone?"

Chelsea rolled her eyes. "He's a smart man, Si. He figured it out a long time ago."

He had to admit that he was fascinated by the argument between the two of them. He didn't understand all of it, but it was definitely intriguing. Big Tag seemed so very calm, collected even in the face of losing his brother the year before. What was really happening underneath that placid surface?

And he had figured out who Chelsea worked for. "If Langley doesn't want people to know there's an employee working here, they shouldn't send out all the suits."

Weston sighed. "That's the business side of the Agency. They're a pain in the arse and they never seem to leave her alone."

"Yeah, well, my new handler is quite the pain in the ass, too. I thought Ten was bad," Chelsea admitted.

"He's going to find his job very short lived if he doesn't stop flirting with you," Weston admitted before turning to Flynn. "Mr. White doesn't wear a suit and you'll never see him coming. He's the truly dangerous one."

"And he's shutting me out," Chelsea complained. "I swear Satan made some kind of deal with him and I'm going to figure it out."

"You will leave it alone and we're going to have a talk about it later. Are you going to help our friend or should we begin that discussion now?" Weston's tone had gone arctic.

The man had the Dom voice down. It sounded particularly good with a British accent.

Should he have turned that voice on Amy earlier today? Should he have sat her down and explained that he wouldn't accept another second of her company's interferences?

Chelsea seemed to calm down and got back to the job at hand. "Do you suspect she manipulated the system to get into your house?"

He didn't simply suspect it. It was a pain in his gut. "Yes. It would be easy. There were only three other Doms going into training. She's got some very close connections at Sanctum."

Weston shook his head. "I don't know. Kai can be remarkably difficult to manipulate. He's a stubborn chap, and despite what my wife will tell you, Kai has the final say when it comes to the training program. Wade might run it, but Kai sets up the couples. Ian merely signs off. If Kai put you together with her, it's because he thinks you'll work well together."

"And if she'd studied him and had a working knowledge of psychology, she could say all the right things," Chelsea said. She was working on her own laptop, her fingers moving. "Her degree is from Wharton, but Wharton is inside the University of Penn system. Ah, there it is. She took a lot of psych courses. Huh, she probably has enough classes for a dual degree. I wonder why she didn't get it?"

Psych was necessary for a truly rounded business degree. Many HR reps had backgrounds in psych. He'd taken a few classes himself, almost all based in business. It taught the student how to read body language, how to negotiate with a variety of people.

She would know how to manipulate him.

"Darling, why don't you do that magic you do and check into her Sanctum application." Weston's voice became soothing as he turned to Flynn. "What did you say to Wade and Kai about your work situation?"

"I didn't exactly go into the feud between our companies and I don't advertise it. We keep these kinds of things very quiet. I don't like talking about the fact that I'm technically the head of my father's company. I prefer to focus on the code I write. When they asked me what my job was I gave them my real work. I'm in programming and R and D. And she's not using her real name. Now that was an oversight. She used a fake name."

Chelsea's fingers were flying across her laptop keys. She'd brought her own system in, plugging it into his. Her eyes were on the screen as she spoke. "I've got her application pulled up here. And her divorce papers. God, I love lower level government systems. I can sneeze on them and get in. Nope. She started the process before her divorce."

He wasn't buying that. "She knew she was getting a divorce and she knew she was changing her name. Did she or did she not legally change her name?"

Chelsea frowned. "She did, but she changed it back right after the divorce."

She'd married Frankie Lyndon for mysterious reasons. Why would she change her name if she'd known it wasn't forever? One more mystery.

"According to the paperwork she filed recently, she requested that the name on her Sanctum membership be changed legally to Slaten," Chelsea continued.

Yet she'd introduced herself as Lyndon.

He'd woken up only hours ago and for a moment he'd panicked that she was gone. He'd checked the bathroom and then gone looking for her. He'd been prepared to find a damn note saying she'd taken a cab. The whole time he'd planned how he would smack that pretty ass of hers for disobeying direct orders. They had still been playing. He'd been specific.

Then he'd found her staring at his computer screen.

He didn't buy her story for a second. She'd known exactly which one to use. She'd gone right past the laptop with its Internet connection and straight for his work system.

"I do find it odd that she didn't have a reaction to your name," Weston mused. "One would think if the atmosphere between your two companies is as bad as you say it is, she would have protested. You have to think she's hiding something."

"I might not have told her my full name."

Weston's brow arched.

The Brit knew how to make a man feel bad. "I have never gone by my legal name. Since I was a kid and wanted to get out of the path set for me, I've gone by Flynn and not John. That was my father's name. I loved the man, but it was sometimes hard to be his son. There were a ton of expectations that went with being John Adler, Jr."

Taking over Glendale, being the boss. He'd never wanted to run the company. He hadn't been particularly good at it the few months he'd tried. He wasn't a big picture guy. He liked to focus on the little things. One thing at a time. It was what he was good at.

Unfortunately, it appeared Chase had taken after him and not their father. Chase was all about history right now. He was obsessed with the subject and showed no signs of wanting to go to business school.

"So you introduced yourself as Flynn and nothing more?" There was a hint of accusation in Weston's tone.

He practically winced. "John Flynn. It's most of my name."

"So you're a dumbass," Chelsea said with a grin. "I love watching a really good dumbass fuck up. I'm hitting your system right now, but who wants to bet me that this baby is pure as the driven snow?"

It wouldn't prove anything except that she hadn't had time to try to crack it. She'd known where to go and how to get there.

"Did she give you an excuse for being on your system?" Weston asked.

"She told me she was trying to e-mail work to tell them she'd be late." And he had a defense he hadn't used yet. "Also, she claims that she's just a worker bee. When I asked her what she does for a living she said she was a corporate drone and it was too boring to talk about. She didn't want me to know she heads Slaten."

"Or she's a female CEO who has to protect her reputation and you're an unknown quantity," Chelsea snapped back. "Do you have any idea how hard it is to crack that glass ceiling? Let me tell you the only thing that's harder. Having to live and work there after you've cracked it."

He could still remember how she'd shuddered in his arms—not from orgasm but from crying. He'd been able to feel the relief rolling off her as she'd cried the night before. What would it be like for a woman as sensitive as Amy appeared to be to always have to have a mask in place? Would a woman like that come to a place like Sanctum seeking relief? Would she seek out a Dom who she could shed her mask for? Would she enjoy submitting because she was in control all of the rest of the time?

Chelsea frowned.

"What is it, darling?" Weston seemed to know when his wife switched from lecture back to work.

"Flynn's password is damn near impossible to crack. I should know. I helped him with it. He's using a system Adam and I designed. It's a full-operations security system that we're about to patent the process for. But I wonder." She pushed the chair back and got down on the ground. "We're so connected to the cyber world that we often forget about the physical."

A chill went through his system.

"Damn," she said. "You should see this."

Flynn moved in, followed by Weston, both looking down at the computer he wrote code on. It was a custom-made PC encased in a big silver tower. Unlike a solid-state drive, this system could switch out different parts and drives. He liked the ease of functionality.

Someone else looked like they'd tried to check out the inside of his system, too. There were distinct scratch marks on the side closest to the desk.

"I would bet that was either a knife or a screwdriver," Weston said with a sigh.

He kept a small screwdriver on his desk. It hadn't been missing this morning but then he hadn't been silent. He'd walked through the condo looking for her. She'd seemed startled, but perhaps she'd had time to get back up into the chair and play out her ruse.

"Do you know if these marks were here before?" Chelsea asked. "When was the last time you changed out drives or worked on the system?"

"It was over a month ago and that was when I switched out the tower casing. It was pristine. I haven't touched it since." His stomach turned.

Weston stood and suddenly there was a small notepad in his hand. He'd pulled it and a pen from his suit pocket. "How many people have been in this condo in the last month? That you know of? I'll contact building management and see if anyone's entered for any reason. We had a structural check on the windows of our place after the last hailstorm hit."

He'd had the same check done. "But I was here for that. I have a maid service, but I'm usually here." His head was reeling. Someone had tried to steal his hard drive. "My brothers have been in here. You and Chelsea, but I can't think of anyone else. No. I had some people from Glendale in about three weeks ago. Three members of the board and my CEO were out this way for a conference and I had them up for dinner and to show them the progress on the code. But those are the last people who would want anything to go wrong with that code. They stand to make a lot of money if we can get it to market."

"Or they could make more money if they sold it to a rival company." Chelsea got back into her seat. "I'll check the dark web and see if there's any buzz about the code you're writing. If someone's going to sell it, that's where the buyers will be. If there's nothing…well, I'm sure someone would rather keep it then."

He glanced at the clock. He was supposed to pick Amy up in less than an hour. He was going to pick her up, take her back to her place, and then bring her here.

Did he dare?

"Chelsea, could you set up a camera around the desk that wouldn't be noticeable?"

Chelsea never looked up from her screen. "Of course. I am the queen. I can do anything."

97

"Do it. I'll pay your consultation fee."

Chelsea simply grinned. "Oh, I catch assholes for free. Also, you bought the pizza last time. I owe you, buddy. Jesse eats a lot. I should have warned you about that before you offered."

"No, you should have warned me that I would get involved in an hour-long debate about the miracles of Harry Potter with Phoebe." Now that he thought about it, Chelsea did owe him.

"Can I talk to you for a moment, Flynn?" Weston asked, gesturing back toward the front of the condo.

Chelsea didn't look up from her work, so Flynn followed Weston.

"Are you sure this is her?" Weston asked, his face grave. "I need you to be fairly certain before you make any kinds of accusations or before you do something foolish like begin a sexual relationship with her."

He must have flushed because the big Brit cursed under his breath.

Flynn sighed. "She's my training sub. We're all going at it from what I can tell. Most of us. You know how it is. It's a very intimate relationship."

"Yes, which is precisely why you should have dropped out of the program the minute you understood what was going on. The minute you figured out a mistake had been made, you should have brought it to Wade's attention."

"I tried." Though not very hard.

"He didn't listen."

"No. I was going to tell him and then…"

Weston sighed. "You saw her. They were right, weren't they? She's a good match for you."

In every way. She matched him intellectually and their needs seemed to dovetail. He needed her affection and she needed someone to take care of her. He needed her warmth and she desperately needed an outlet for all that love she had. He could soak it up like a fucking sponge.

But he couldn't simply allow her to use him.

"Yes," he admitted. "She's practically perfect for me. I can't think of a woman I've wanted more than her. Maybe it's just the training program."

"It could be. Your first sub is always special. There's a shared intimacy that tends to bond you, but you have to think about the fact that she's got deep connections to the club. If you screw her over, you piss off a lot of people."

Including his brother's best friend.

"I'm not going to accuse her of anything without proof. And I'll be the happiest man on the planet if it's not her. I told you. I want to be serious about this woman. I can't, though, if she's spying on me. I can't walk away either."

"I'll very quietly investigate," Weston offered. "And Chelsea can place cameras and security devices in a way no one will recognize. If the person who tried to get inside the tower comes back, we'll catch them, but have you thought about the fact that eventually she's going to have to know your real name?"

He wasn't even thinking about that now. There was too much else to worry about. "I'll deal with it when I have to."

"And what happens if someone mentions who you work for at Sanctum?"

"I don't know why they would. Most people have no idea I'm connected to Glendale because I'm not actively working for corporate." He didn't like the implication that he was hiding something. He wasn't. "I do write code for a living."

Weston huffed slightly, an oddly elegant sound. "Yes, and I can afford this place because of the riches I made from MI6."

"He totally got all his cash from my former criminal ventures." Chelsea proved that they could move away, but she could still hear.

"Such rubbish." But Weston gave his wife a wink. "Amy's got to be curious about how you afford this place."

"She hasn't asked. Not at all." Because she was being polite or because she knew the truth? "If she does, I'll explain that my father was a wealthy man and leave it at that. I don't suspect you go into how your family owns a good portion of England."

"No, I don't."

"He had a relative who got his head cut off for screwing around with Anne Boleyn," Chelsea said cheerfully. "I mention that all the time."

"Yes, well, luckily we Westons were a fertile lot. We did seem to get executed quite a bit. I should never have allowed Chelsea to spend time with my mother. She thought it would do her new daughter-in-law good to hear all the family stories. She wanted Chelsea to know what a noble line she was marrying into. Sadly, all my wife was interested in were the criminals and philanderers."

"Hey, I told your mom all about my Russian mobster family," Chelsea offered cheerfully.

"Yes, it's the only time I've seen my mother faint."

"That was not about my family. That was the caviar. I'm certain it was bad. It tasted horrible. Why can't anyone in your family simply make a grilled cheese? Lunch is like fifteen courses long."

They were off, bickering in their affectionate way.

And he missed Amy. Despite what had happened this morning, he felt the hours they'd spent apart.

What the hell was he going to do if he found out she was lying?

And what would he do if she wasn't?

* * * *

Amy was glad she wasn't on the computer with Frankie. He'd called in but she'd put him on speakerphone instead of Skype. It was a good thing or he would likely see the ridiculously silly grin on her face.

"I like him."

His golden voice came over the line. "Yes, I can hear that in your voice. And you said his name was Flynn, right?"

Oh, he wasn't pulling that trick on her. She knew exactly what he would do if he had a full name. There would be a PI on Flynn's ass before they hung up the phone. "Yes, and that's all you're getting out of me, mister. I know your tricks all too well. I don't want you running some kind of security check on my new boyfriend."

There was a pause on the line. "I thought you said this was casual."

Yes, so glad they weren't staring at each other over a screen or he would have seen her blush. "It is. I misspoke. Honestly, we've only had a couple of dates."

And the hottest night of her life. After the weirdness of Flynn catching her trying to use his computer, he'd gone right back to crazy sexy lover mode. He'd tossed her on his bed and he hadn't let her up for hours. He'd devoured her like a starving man. She could still feel his hands on her.

"Dates? I thought he was your training Dom. You're supposed to see him in class for the first few weeks and then in the club."

When had he gotten so particular about the rules? Of which there were none at Sanctum. They were very much "live and let fuck." "We've been out to dinner a few times. Sanctum isn't like your club. They're all friends so they don't have such rigid rules about contact among trainees."

"Well, maybe they should. You don't know this man. I don't know this man. Does your sister know him?"

She shouldn't have said anything beyond it was going nicely and she was enjoying the class. "Bridget doesn't know him, but he's Will's best friend's brother, and Flynn and Will seem to get along well."

At least they had in the ER when they were working in tandem to treat her like an invalid.

"I like Will. He's got a good head on his shoulders, but with the baby coming and him being promoted to head of Neurosurgery, I don't think he can properly look after you."

She felt her hands clench. She hated that idea. That she needed to be looked after. Like she wasn't competent.

Except with Flynn. He hadn't treated her like she wasn't smart enough to take care of herself. She'd been hurt and he'd been there to make things easier for her. He'd taken care of her and let her take care of him. That had felt like real caring. A true exchange of affections.

"Don't. Don't treat me like I don't have a brain in my head." She'd had far too much of that to last a lifetime. No matter what she'd done, her father had treated her as incompetent. The only reason he'd promoted her up the ranks was she had the name Slaten. If there had been a brother around she wouldn't have been encouraged to go to school at all. There were still members of her board who thought because she didn't have a penis she couldn't properly run the company. She couldn't handle it coming from Frankie.

"Hey." His voice lowered and though she couldn't see him, she could practically feel his hand on hers. "I didn't mean it that way."

She knew he was trying to protect her, but his version of protection would be selecting a date for her and ensuring that he treated her properly. Frankie couldn't help himself. When he loved, he tended to try to take over.

But she wasn't his wife or his lover or his soul mate. She'd loved him, did love him, but she needed to make her own decisions about her love life. She'd been strong enough to take the company away from her father, strong enough to move them across the country and press on with her vision. She had to be strong enough to risk her heart for the right man.

"You did," she replied, but with a softer tone. "You think I'm naïve about men. You know I've had some sex in my time. I'm not exactly a virgin."

"Yes, but that was all about pleasure, my darling girl," he replied with a long sigh. "If I thought for a second you were simply enjoying this man, I wouldn't say a thing. When it comes to love, you've only really had one of those and he proved to be so very inadequate."

Tears threatened. Something about being able to cry the night before had made her more emotional this afternoon. Opening up to Flynn had made her more vulnerable to everything. "You weren't inadequate, Frankie. You just couldn't love me back."

"Loving you wasn't the problem. I love you so much it hurts."

Her heart ached, but she'd dealt with this a very long time ago. She'd known her first love wouldn't, couldn't be her last.

"All right, you couldn't love me the way I need to be loved." She often thought that Frankie would have been perfectly happy staying married to her. He would have enjoyed living with her, being her companion. Oh, he would have had a boy on the side, but he could have been happy. They'd made their arrangement for business purposes, but she'd seen his sadness when she'd moved out.

She needed more.

"Does it help that I wish I could?" He was quiet for a moment. "I'll never find a male version of you and I don't know that I can be happy without it. So I'm being selfish because I don't want to lose you. You can't know how important you are to me."

She could because she felt the same way. "I love you too, Frankie. But I need you to stop being my protector and be my friend. Stop trying to figure out whether Flynn is good for me and accept that he's in my life."

There was a pause on the line and then the sound of him sighing.

"All right. I can do that on the romance front, but you can't expect me to do it on the business side. I've heard some rumors."

Rumors were the bane of her existence, but still it was nice to talk about something they could agree on. "Of what?"

"Glendale is meeting with Clannahan."

The whole room seemed to go cold. Of all the things she wanted to hear, the very last was Glendale having anything at all to do with the Irish company she was courting. "Why the hell would they meet with Clannahan?"

"No idea, but that's the word on the street," Frankie replied. "Glendale is looking to buy a couple of smaller companies. From what I understand, they're looking for a company to help handle some new product they're developing. Do you know anything about that?"

"I try to stay as far away from Glendale as I can."

"Sweetheart, you have to have some sources. You need to figure out what they want from Clannahan. If that means you have to use some of your father's old connections, you might think about it. It seems to me that Glendale is still up to its old tricks. How else would they have known about Clannahan? It's a tiny Irish firm with very few connections to the States right now."

"But they have some very innovative processes when it comes to delivery. It's precisely why I want to work with them." But she couldn't afford to buy them. A merger was what she was looking for.

And yet they were so small. Glendale would need a larger firm. One on US soil. The only reason for them talking to Clannahan was to fuck with Slaten.

If Glendale swooped in and took her prize…she had no idea what she would do.

She took a deep breath. She would simply find another way. She wouldn't give up. She would never give up fighting for this company and the workers who had shown her such kindness when she was younger, the ones who depended on her now.

She needed to regroup. If they were trying to steal Clannahan, she needed to figure out where her leak was and how to plug it.

There was a brief knock on her door and then it opened. Val scrambled in.

"I'm so sorry. I couldn't stop him."

"Babe, I'm going to have to call you back," she said grimly as her father strode in. Before Frankie could say anything she hung up because she couldn't spare another second.

The devil was in the room and he demanded all of her attention or he would work his way into some kind of trouble.

"I thought I had barred you from the building." She forced her whole body to go icy cold. There was no room for anger or real emotion with the man who'd sired her. "Val, could you please call security for me?"

"Don't bother." Her father was dressed in what had to be a thousand dollar suit and designer loafers. "I'll leave as soon as I've explained to you that I'm back on the board. Here's the judge's ruling that states plainly the tape that fucker Taggart took of me isn't admissible in a court of law."

She watched as he placed a folder on her desk. She didn't bother to open it. A phalanx of lawyers would have already gone through it. She was certain that urgent message from legal had something to do with this. It had come in from California earlier this morning, but she'd been busy with Flynn and then she'd called Frankie.

"I'll have them argue that California legal standards have nothing to do with our bylaws. The corporate bylaws were written by you."

His mouth spread in a shark's grin. "Yes, I believe my lawyers covered that in the case. Legally you can remove me as the CEO because those bylaws were in effect then. I wasn't arguing that. I was arguing that you couldn't force me to sell stock I owned. You'll find Andrew and Aunt Vespa have given the stock back to me. I can now own stock since you changed the bylaws."

She'd changed the bylaws because they'd been draconian. Oh, she'd used them to oust her father. He'd had a set of strict morality clauses that he'd broken on a daily basis, but used as a whip to put fear into everyone else and bring them into line.

She'd counted on her relatives greed. Originally he'd been forced to divest himself of all stock. Apparently he'd sold it to relatives who'd simply held it until he was ready to spring his trap.

Damn it. Now she would have to deal with the snake in the grass at every board meeting.

How much cash did she have? She could likely buy out her

cousins. They were always looking for a quick buck and they tended to not be smart enough to know what financial security really meant. There was also the public stock. She would have to take a look at that.

"Well, then the board meetings should be a blast from now on, Dad."

His eyes looked vaguely reptilian as he regarded her. Like a snake about to strike. "You know, I underestimated you."

"You tend to do that with women."

"I didn't realize how much you'd learned from the old man. You've even managed to put the company in the position where when I get it back, I won't be able to sell it. Not for a while. Touché, dear daughter. You know if I'd realized you would be more loyal to the idiots who work for us, I would never have allowed you to intern."

"Why on earth would I show any loyalty to you?" She was pleased with how cold the question came out.

He chuckled as though he found the question endlessly amusing. Very likely he did since he wouldn't understand what loyalty meant if he was staring at the definition. "Because I raised you, little girl. I brought you in and taught you, and now I'm going to teach you another lesson. I'm going to take this company back and I'm going to ruin you. When I'm done, no one will hire you. I'll get the company back where it needs to be and then I'll sell it. All you did was put off my plans. You didn't ruin them. And thank you for bringing the company here. The taxes are so low. I'll make a fortune. Don't expect to be in my will."

"Don't expect me to let go without a fight."

Luckily that was the moment security showed up. Two big men in dark uniforms entered the room. Bill and Carl. They were nice men with families. They worked the day shift and came in early because she so often did. When she'd realized they came in before their shifts started so she wouldn't be alone in the building, she'd made sure there was coffee and some overtime pay for the two.

"Is this man bothering you, Ms. Slaten?" Carl asked, his voice deep.

This man? He knew exactly who was standing in the room. She kind of loved them both in that moment. "Yes, he is. I think he should definitely leave. Perhaps you could escort him and make sure he finds his way out."

Bill nodded. "Yeah, Ms. Slaten. We can do that. We wouldn't want him hanging around."

If her father was bothered, he didn't show it. He shrugged. "Well, you won't be able to keep me away from the board meetings, Amy. I wonder what the rest of the board will think about your newest venture? Really, did you think I wouldn't find out about the Sanctum thing? How will the board react when they know you're a fucking pervert? Sweet little Amy is involved in a sex club."

She felt her cheeks flame, but she refused to back down. "I don't care what they think of my personal life."

"Time to go," Carl bit out, moving in.

Her father's smile was chilling. "They will care, Amy. Whether or not there's a morality clause, you know what they'll think of you and you know it will affect how they see you. I'll make sure they know everything that goes on at that club. Don't expect them to look you in the eye again. I'll make sure everyone here knows what a whore you are."

Bill nodded her way as he started to follow her father out of the room. Carl closed the door behind him and she was left alone with her assistant.

"Ms. Slaten? Are you all right?" Val asked.

She wanted to cry. It was all falling apart. Her father could hurt her. She could hurt the club if her father decided to go public with what he knew. Had he been following her?

Could he hurt Flynn?

"I'm fine." She ensured her face was perfectly placid.

"No one will care," Val said quietly. "Well, some of them will because they'll want to know where the club is. Is it one of those ones like in your sister's books? Are the men really attractive?"

Amy was so startled she laughed. "You're married."

Val grinned a little. "Yes, I'm married, not dead." She sobered a bit. "Don't let him stop you. Every single employee here knows what you sacrificed to save their jobs. We love you, Ms. Slaten, no matter how you choose to relax. But seriously, what about the men?"

She was eased somewhat by her assistant's kind words. "They're spectacular. Every single one of them."

But one in particular was amazing.

Was she going to have to choose between her career and Flynn?

"And Val? What's up with the 'Ms. Slaten'?" She'd never asked her assistant to call her that. She was much less formal than her father. The only time Val called her Ms. Slaten was around clients.

Val huffed slightly. "That man doesn't get to call you anything but Ms. Slaten. I don't think he should be allowed to hear your first name. Ever."

At least she had allies. "I was named after that man's mother."

"I hope she was nicer than he was."

Her grandmother. She'd been a lovely woman who lived out her last years in a gorgeous beachfront house in Malibu. When she was well she would bring Amy and Bridget out to visit.

The one thing you can't ever give up on is yourself, my darling.

Those had been the last words she'd heard from her grandmother. She took a deep breath.

"Val, I'm going to need you to call a few people in. We've got some work to do. Bring my lawyer in first. And get me everything we have on Padraig and Seamus Clannahan."

There had to be something she could do. She couldn't win a money battle with Glendale, but sometimes these small family companies valued other things. If there was a way in, she was going to find it.

It was time to get ready. She was going to war.

She had to wonder what price she would be forced to pay to win.

Chapter Six

Flynn frowned and set his phone back in his locker.

Bear, who had the locker next to him, closed his door with absolutely no sound. For a man named after a grizzly, he moved like a panther. "You alone again tonight?"

It had been a solid two weeks since the morning he'd found Amy sitting at his desk and he was frustrated more and more every day that passed. "Yes. She's working late. It's the second time this week. I have to talk to Wade to figure out if she can even complete the class with two absences. I would call her and discuss it, but she's in a meeting."

She'd been in a lot of meetings this week. When she was in bed with him, he could feel how close they were. When they weren't, there was a distance he couldn't seem to shake.

"They'll let you do make ups." The massive dude adjusted his vest. "Lucy had to cover for a friend's shift at Top last week. I sat in and then went over the materials with her in private. Wade was cool once he'd ensured I properly passed on the lesson. So don't worry about that. I think we're working on role-play tonight and how to handle your partner's needs even if they don't match your own."

He was beginning to wonder about her needs. "That should be interesting. How's it going with you and Lucy?"

Bear grinned. "She's a pistol. I mean it. She has a couple. I was worried about it at first because I've been around some chicks with really crazy eyes, but apparently her father is ex-military and believes in his baby girl being able to protect herself."

"Yeah, Regina has more guns than I do," Vaughn admitted. "But she's third generation DPD. Let me tell you we're going to do some serious role-play in her squad car. I'm totally looking forward to that."

"So you're both pretty happy with your subs?" He was curious. He'd spent most of his time alone with Amy. She'd gotten her car back from the shop the day before. He'd had her all to himself at night for two solid weeks.

For the whole time she'd followed his rules. After that first night, she'd packed a suitcase and stayed with him. He took her to and from work, to class on Sanctum nights. He'd taken her to dinner a few times and she'd cooked when they stayed in. She'd gone over to Simon and Chelsea's with him to watch a movie. It had been a spy thriller and the other couple had playfully bickered about how unrealistic it was, but Amy had cuddled up in his lap and she'd fallen asleep. He'd carried her back to the condo and made love to her the next morning.

He knew he should think of it as sex. Lots of dirty, filthy, hot sex, but it felt like something more. The sex was beyond fantastic.

Not once had he found her sniffing around his computer. He'd stayed in bed long past when she would get up and every day he'd carefully checked the surveillance footage. Nothing.

Except the fact that she sang to herself sometimes. She did a mean Katy Perry and she talked to her ex-husband on the phone. Apparently Frankie Hollywood got up super early to work out and they talked every morning.

She knew about Clannahan and something was up with her board. His CEO assured him Clannahan was going to agree to a friendly buyout and they would have the assets they needed, but the Irishmen were still coming to Dallas to meet with Slaten.

He felt like a shit that he'd listened to her side of that conversation. Even more of a shit because he'd heard her confess to her ex that she'd never had it so good with another man. She'd told him that it was still casual but she was hoping for more.

Why would she tell her ex that? Why would she pretend with him?

Now she was pulling away from him. He could feel it.

Bear shrugged his big shoulders. "Lucy's a good kid."

"Regina and I get along nicely," Vaughn said.

"You sleeping with her?"

Vaughn's brow rose. "Am I in the wrong locker room?"

Bear chuckled. "You better get used to it. When the MT boys are around it's gossip central in here. Oh, Big Tag will pretend he's all about the sports and shit then he'll sit you down and start in on what team will go all the way and bam, suddenly you're talking about some issue that's going on and he's pretending to vomit, but he keeps on you and then your problem's solved and you go take a shower because you feel dirty. And yet you also feel pretty good because you kind of know what to do."

Vaughn frowned. "That's a lot to take in. Brighton told me this place was cool. Now you're saying there's some sort of crazy fix-it guy who makes you talk about your hookups?"

"No. I'm saying that the guys are all friends and they kind of lean on each other," Bear explained. "You don't work for McKay-Taggart as closely as I do. It's definitely got that weird family vibe. They help each other out. I think that's what Flynn's trying to do. He's not being nosy. He wants to talk about the fact that he is sleeping with his sub."

"Why would I care if he's sleeping with his sub?" Vaughn asked.

Bear shook his head. "There's a reason you're friends with Boomer."

Wow. He'd stepped into that one. He didn't want to get Vaughn and Bear into some kind of argument. "Forget I asked. Don't worry about it. Who's teaching tonight? Is it Wade or one of the partners?"

Bear looked like he wanted to push the subject, but he finally sighed and let it go. "It's Jake Dean and Adam Miles and their sub, Serena. Apparently she's very good with role-play, but don't expect more than a lecture. She's seriously pregnant. There's a lot of that going on in this place. Use double protection, man. I think something's in the water."

Vaughn shivered as though he couldn't think of anything worse and strode away.

Bear turned back to Flynn. "Don't mind him. He's younger than the rest of us in more ways than age. And no, I'm not sleeping with Lucy and I'm not going to. She's a good kid, but she's a little more innocent than what I'm looking for."

"So you think Kai and Wade got it wrong?" From the second he'd seen Amy he'd known he couldn't keep his hands off her.

Bear frowned. "Maybe not. I like her. A lot. But I'm not in any kind of place to offer her anything. She's not looking for a full-time Dom either. She's working her way through college and just wants to have some fun."

"Why not have fun with you?"

Bear smiled. "Because I'm too rough for her, but I'm also not going to hurt her feelings about it. I think that's why we were teamed up. Kai knew I would come to view her as a friend and that she could push some of her boundaries with me. I'll be patient with her and not take advantage. I think it's different with you and Amy. Me and Lucy are truly not looking for anything serious. You want a committed sub."

He was starting to be afraid he wanted more than a sub. He was starting to wonder if he didn't want a wife. A very specific wife. "I'm at a place in my life where it makes sense to be in a more committed relationship."

Bear nodded. "And Amy seems like a woman who wants to be happy. I think they did a good job with the two of you. And for the record, Vaughn and Regina are going at it like rabbits, and that man is in pretty deep. I caught him looking at gun accessories to buy her for graduation day."

He had to smile at the thought. What would Amy want?

A collar. A really gorgeous collar that would allow every man who looked at her to see she was taken.

That might be more for him than her.

A week at some ridiculous resort where he could pamper her and feed her and love her and get that worried look out of her eyes.

"It's good to know I'm not the only one."

"If you want to talk or anything, we could go and get a beer sometime. I'll see you out there." Bear walked away and he was alone in the locker room.

What the hell was he doing? He was practically asking the other guys for relationship therapy. It wasn't like him. He was private. How could he be so upset that he wasn't going to spend the night with her? He was actually getting pissy that a woman he'd known for less than a month had chosen to work late.

Was she working on the Clannahan deal? Was she trying to snake that company out from under him?

Did she need it? How bad had things gotten at Slaten?

"No sub for you tonight?" a deep voice asked.

He turned and recognized Jake Dean. He was one of the founding members of Sanctum and taught several of the classes. "It looks like it. Amy texted me an hour ago. She's stuck in a meeting. Bear told me I just have to sit through the class and then go over it with her."

"That's fine." Dean moved to his locker. "It's more of a lecture on how sometimes your partner will come up with some crazy shit and you gotta find a way to accommodate her. Or him. We're simply using the idea of role-playing because we all had to get used to Phoebe and Jesse doing weird wizard sex things. Don't even ask. And we've got some super geeks. I had to watch the Avengers have an orgy a couple of weeks back. I was cool with it until they brought in Thor's hammer. That kind of freaked me out."

Amy would make a super hot Black Widow. He could catch her and go all Hulk on her pretty backside. "Yeah, that sounds weird."

Jake frowned his way as though he'd known what Flynn was thinking. "You're one of them, aren't you? You're one of those geeks who doesn't look like a geek but you know way too much about comic books to be normal."

He shrugged. "Geek is the new chic. I'm afraid my sub's into it, too. You should probably expect some *Buffy the Vampire Slayer* role-playing. And *Dart*. She loves *Dart*."

He would have to get that costume and she could play the pretty hacker who aided Dart in all his efforts, and he could need some sexual healing after a long mission. Yeah, that sounded good.

Dean shook his head. "No. No. It's the only thing that's completely forbidden at Sanctum. It makes Kai sick. Sorry, the dude who plays Dart is Kai's brother and he's famously prudish about his brother. I guess when you're bombarded daily with how hot your baby brother is you get defensive. It's kind of like Adam has to deal with me."

There was a vomiting sound from two rows over.

Dean waved it off. "Don't mind him. He's got sympathy nausea. You know I could tell you that the best way to deal with her missing this class is some real world play. Is your sub interested at all in role-play?"

From what he could tell she was a little into it. She'd mentioned the Viking thing more than once. "I think she could go for it."

It would get her out of her head for a while. It might put a smile on her face.

"Then that's what you should do," Dean explained.

Adam Miles moved around the row of lockers. He was dressed in his leathers and shaking his head at his partner. "Seriously? I'm far more attractive than you are."

"You keep thinking that, buddy," Dean said with a sigh. "Flynn, take my advice. Grab your girl or you might end up with a hanger-on."

"Hanger-on?" Miles shot back. "Dude, you wouldn't have any idea how to make it through a day without me, much less how to take care of Serena and our son. And don't listen to this asshole. Like I showed up and latched on. You wouldn't be here without me. You were a complete asshole when we first got together with Serena. You needed me to smooth over all those accusations you leveled at her."

Dean laughed. "Hah. I fixed that with pure determination, brother. I fucked up but I wasn't letting that woman or you getting your mansies stop us."

Did he dare ask? "Mansies?"

"Man period." Adam shot his partner the finger. "And my mansies were way more productive than your steroidal rage at the world that had done you wrong. He actually accused our sweet wife of pretending to have a stalker as a publicity stunt."

Dean shrugged. "Yeah, well, I took that shit right back after the bullets started flying. That wasn't what pissed Serena off. It was accusing her of sleeping with us to further her plot that really got the old engine going. Let me tell you, you've got it easy buddy. Getting matched up by experts and having a nice six weeks in a safe place to get to know her...that's the dream. We did it with stalkers and guns and knives."

Miles smiled. "Damn, man. Good times."

"You know it, brother." He shared a smile with his partner before turning back to Flynn. "Take the night off. Go to her apartment and set up a scene. If she's had to work all night, she's likely stressed and tired and in need of some fun. With a surprise scene, the key is to figure out what your sub needs. Does she need the play? Or does she need you to scrap it all and rub her feet and feed her dinner? That's what I'm going to talk about tonight. Naturally there are times when the Dom needs the sub to be flexible. I can talk to her about that on another night."

Flynn shook his head. "She's got that lesson down. She's fallen into the role of making sure I have breakfast and lunch and that I pull my head out of cyberspace for a while and relax."

"Then it sounds like you're on the right path," Miles assured him. "Are you still sure this is the right lifestyle for you?"

There was no doubt in his mind. "We'll never be twenty-four seven, but I think we both like having our roles and clearly defined goals for what we need and want. We're quite compatible in that fashion. I don't want a sub I have to make decisions for. Hell, sometimes I like it when Amy takes charge of what's going on in real life. I get caught up in work. She gets caught up in work."

"So you need to understand your roles will be more fluid than others," Dean explained. "Our wife is the single most talented person I've ever met and yet she's at her best when she's got nothing to worry about except our son and her writing. We handle the rest of the world so she doesn't have to. We make the decisions in our daily lives. She deals with her work. We all sit down as a family and make the big decisions. You and Amy need to figure out what works for you. The key is not letting things slide. You have to talk to her about her needs and your needs. You have to treat your relationship like something worth putting real time and effort into. That's the nature of the entire class."

"That doesn't sound like simple D/s." It sounded like a damn fine way to have a marriage.

"That's the beauty of D/s. It's not only about one thing. It means being honest about what we want and need and finding the proper partners to make it happen. It works for business, friendship, play. It definitely works for marriage," Miles finished.

"So go forth and set up a surprise for your girl." Dean started moving to the exit. "I'll handle Wade. We'll call it make-up homework. Have fun."

Miles hung back. "The honesty thing is the important part. You understand that, right?"

"Yes." He got the feeling Miles wasn't simply reiterating theory.

"Good." Miles stared at him for a moment and then started to turn.

"You know." The words were out before he could stop them.

"I know everything. It's a sad fact of my life. I'm very good at putting things together," Miles explained. "I had Hutch run the background checks. He's a smart kid, but utterly uninterested in anything except candy and first-person shooters. He can find every piece of data, but he rarely puts puzzles together. I like to try to guess who Kai's going to pair up. The last two training classes have been easier since Big Tag...well, let's just say he's got other things on his mind."

He'd lost his youngest brother. That would put any man off his game. "She used her married name."

"But any background check will show you who she is and what she does. The same as you. I got interested because of all the trainees, you two have the most in common. Vaughn and Regina come from similar backgrounds, cop and ex-military. They tend to go together nicely, but their childhoods diverge to the point that I wonder how they'll mesh long term. Not you and Amy. You have so very, very much in common."

Adam Miles was the communications expert at McKay-Taggart. Unlike Chelsea, who worked for the Agency, he didn't have the same kinds of rules attached to him. He could pretty much do as he pleased. "She doesn't say much about her childhood."

Miles sent him an enigmatic smile. "You'll have to ask her, but I suspect you won't. You haven't talked to her about your mutual interests, have you? Does she know? There's a reason we don't give trainees their partner's dossiers."

No, the club kept that for themselves. All the records were kept private, but the members assumed Kai and Wade and Big Tag wouldn't allow anyone in who could be dangerous. Training partners could get as personal or be as impersonal as they wished.

"I have no idea." He could say that honestly now. If Miles had asked a few weeks ago, he would have qualified that answer with a probably, but now he couldn't.

She seemed so open with him up to a point. She was hiding something now, but he was almost sure it was worry and anxiety, not lies.

Amy was the kind of woman who would try to put a bright face on things. He rather thought it was a leftover from her childhood. Or the result of years of working at a high level in corporate America. The female executives at Glendale were brilliant and innovative and also bore the scars of having to constantly prove they were tough enough. No matter what he did to combat it, the corporate culture reasserted itself time and time again. It was likely better than it had been, but it would take women like Amy fighting and winning to make it truly change.

Damn it. He respected her, admired her.

Miles leaned against the lockers. "I would suspect not. I got to know her a little when she was bringing down her father. She's a very nice woman. Smart. Capable. I can't talk much about it because I do have some rigid guidelines when it comes to privacy. I invade it so very often that I have to keep secrets to myself. Jake and Serena don't understand the rivalry between your companies."

"I don't understand the rivalry between our companies." If Miles could shed some light, he would take it. "My father never explained it to me. I didn't truly understand why he hated George Slaten so much."

"Here's what I've pieced together. Slaten and your father went to college together. At one point in time there were rumors that Slaten wanted to merge with Glendale. Slaten was bigger at the time, but Glendale was coming up in the world. Something happened. Again, I only have rumors. I think your father pulled the plug and they've been going at it ever since. Maybe it simply turned into a rivalry about money, but I suspect Slaten had an affair with your father's first wife and that's what soured the friendship. Not that I think anyone could have truly been friends with Slaten. He's a bastard."

"It makes me wonder how Amy turned out so lovely."

"And quite unlike her sister. Bridget is open and out there with every emotion. Her creativity and vitality are out there for everyone to see. Amy is more of a mystery. Likely because she watched what happened to Bridget when she defied their father. She's more private."

Bridget was a writer. She was expected to be emotional and flamboyant. Amy was expected to be controlled and sedate.

Except she wasn't with him. She let loose and gave him everything she had. She cried with him.

"I've had some issues with spying," Flynn admitted. It seemed like

Miles kept things private. Perhaps he would make a good sounding board. He didn't want Mitch involved any more than he already was. Will Daley was Mitch's best friend and he didn't want to cause them trouble. "Most of those can be traced back to Slaten."

"And now you're worried she's lying to you," Miles summed up. "If it helps, both of your firms hide it quite well. There's not a lot in the press about it unless you know how to read between the lines. It's why it got past Kai and Wade. I didn't pick up on it until after Hutch had sent the reports through. I'm going to give you some advice. Do you care about this woman?"

That was easy. "Yes."

"Do you want to have a relationship with her that goes past the training period?"

Again. No question about that. "I think I want her no matter what she's done."

Miles whistled. "You have to talk to her. It doesn't have to be today, but you better sit down and explain yourself before the course is over and you're regularly around the rest of the club. They'll figure it out and if she finds out from anyone other than you, you're in serious trouble."

"And if she already knows?"

"Then you'll have to decide how to handle it. But I doubt that. She took the company from her father in order to change it, to make it better. Why would she do the same things her father had done?"

"Because sometimes desperate people do desperate things." He'd heard the rumor that her father was causing trouble, trying to get his stock back in a bid to oust Amy.

Gaining access to a piece of software that could revolutionize the way they did business would go a long way to ensuring she kept her place at the company. He'd seen people do more for far less.

He was stuck, but he had some time. They wouldn't go to the club until the last week. He could figure this out.

But tonight he just wanted to be close to her.

"Good luck," Miles said with a tip of his head. "Are you going to find your girl and teach her tonight's lesson?"

At least one thing could go right. "I think that would help us both."

He had to find a way to surprise her. And he would need a few props.

His girl was coming home to a very stern teacher tonight.

* * * *

She had her plan in place. It was like a mantra in her head. Tomorrow she was going to meet with the Clannahan brothers. She'd managed to convince them there was still a chance she could change their minds. It played through the back of her head that they were likely using the meeting with her to get the best deal they could out of Glendale.

But they didn't know that she'd figured out their weakness.

She was putting it all out there. *Please work.* It had to work.

She had a brand new consultant. She prayed he had a job at the end of the day tomorrow. Oh, it was a side job for him, but she wasn't going to tell the Clannahan brothers that.

It was actually quite a desperate play, but she had no idea what else to do. Glendale seemed to know everything she had planned. They'd easily bested her best offer—but not by too much. It was as if they had an insider who knew exactly what they were doing.

She wouldn't put it past her father to do it, though he shouldn't know what their bid was going to be. Hell, she couldn't trust Glendale at all. The rumor was some of her former employees were being paid by Glendale to tell the company all about her.

And then there was her father's nasty plan to take back his position. She had to talk to Flynn. She'd put it off for a while, but she had to tell him and figure out if she was going to ruin his life, too.

The elevator opened and she trudged down the hall. At this time of night, the hall was deserted. She'd missed him so much. She'd sat in her meeting going over and over what they would do tomorrow and Flynn had been there in the back of her mind. She'd wanted to be in his arms, sitting in his lap as they talked about whatever Wade had planned for them.

She had to think about pulling out of the class. Val and the workers might not care, but her board would. She was very much aware of how light her control was. Even if she brought in Clannahan, if she lost two votes, her father could be right back at the head of the company and she would be out.

Would Flynn still want to see her if she couldn't go to Sanctum? Would he be all right with playing in private?

The decision might have been made for her already. She'd missed two classes. Surely they were going to lose patience with her soon and she would be informed that she would need to take the class over again.

Even if they gave her that option, she would decline because she couldn't imagine another training Dom.

She was in too deep with that man. Way too deep.

With a weary sigh, she pressed her key in and unlocked the door. There had been a little hope in the back of her head that Flynn would show up at her building to take her out to a late dinner, but he hadn't even texted her.

He was likely losing patience with her, too.

She stopped in the middle of the doorway because someone had moved her kitchen table and Flynn was sitting there, his big body in slacks, a dress shirt, and a sport coat. He looked up from the book in front of him.

"Ms. Lyndon, it's been brought to my attention that you've been skipping classes. Why don't you come into my office and we'll discuss how to fix this particular situation."

She felt her eyes widen. What the hell? "How did you get into my apartment?"

A single brow rose over his dark eyes. "This is my office but if I were to lock myself out, a friend has a key and would be very happy to let me in. Especially if I need to meet with a wayward student and attempt to show her the discipline she needs to get back on track."

Holy shit. He'd gotten her spare key from Will and Bridget's place. Had he explained that he intended to turn her living room into a professor's office?

Her whole body flushed at the thought. He looked so very stern.

Still, they had more important things to talk about. "Flynn, I think we should…"

"Professor Flynn," he corrected, his eyes narrowing on her. "And there's nothing more important than talking about the recent downturn in your normally excellent work. Tonight's lesson was on role-playing and I believe you need a private tutoring session. Everything else can wait. I'm here for the evening because I am dedicated to ensuring your proper education. So you should lock the door behind you and put away your things. We need to discuss how to deal with your disciplinary issues."

His hand moved across the desk to a ruler. His fingers played along it.

Her heart skipped a beat. Was he planning on using that on her? There was so much going on, but he was offering her a few hours of respite. The day's stress had taken its toll, but he could give her relief in the form of some ridiculously nasty sex.

"And we'll talk afterward?"

He stood and strode over to her, his eyes softening. "We can talk during the play, baby. That's what this is for. You can tell me everything that went wrong with your day and why you're pulling away from me, and you can do all of it while we're playing. Or I can take off this silly coat and put your table back and we'll sit down and simply talk."

Ah, the choice. He was offering her a chance to talk, but also a different way to talk about it. If she sat down with him, she would be academic, unemotional. It was hard to switch gears and she'd had days of forcing herself to be logical and methodical.

But play was different. It gave her a layer of protection and she could let go.

Her father's voice played through her head. She was a pervert to need this. It was wrong. Normal people didn't have to get spanked and tied down to talk about their issues. Normal people didn't pretend to be a schoolgirl so they could fucking cry.

"Don't," he said, cupping her face and forcing her to look at him. "I don't know where you're going in your head, but don't leave me. This is you and me and no one else."

That was what she needed. No one else but him. He was her safe place and she was so scared of losing him. She'd been able to be herself with this man, in a way she'd never been able to with any other person. With her sister she had a role to play. With Frankie there was and always would be the distance of not being physically engaged. No friend or lover had ever made her feel the way Flynn did.

And what the fuck was normal? Her family certainly wasn't. They were awful and judgmental when they had zero right to be. There was nothing wrong with what she and Flynn were doing and she wasn't going to give it up. If they thought for a single second they could bully her, they were wrong.

"I'm so sorry, Professor Flynn. I got caught at the library and I lost track of time. I'm afraid I missed your class, but I did have good reasons. The other professors are loading me down with work." Work was a bitch in other words, but then she'd never been open with him about how difficult her job could be. Maybe this was a way she could broach the subject. "You know I'm an honors student."

His lips curled up slightly in the sexiest of smirks, as though he'd known he would get his way. Arrogant, gorgeous man. "You won't be an honor student for long if you can't pass my class. Do as I asked and lock the door. I wouldn't want other students interrupting our time together."

She did as he asked and when she turned he was back at his desk, gesturing for her to join him.

Some of the tension of the day slid away from her. They had hours to play. Tomorrow she would meet with Clannahan and roll the dice, but tonight, she didn't have to think about it anymore.

Tonight she could focus on pleasing her horny professor.

She put her laptop bag and her purse down. "Please, Professor Flynn. You know I can't let my grade point average slip. I might lose my scholarship. I can't possibly disappoint my parents like that."

"I might be able to let you make up the class you missed, but you have to understand that I can't allow it to go without punishment."

Yeah, she was totally counting on his punishment. Her nipples were already hard. "What kind of punishment, Sir? Should I help you rearrange your books? Or perhaps you need an assistant with your lower level classes."

He studied her. "Perhaps, but first we should deal with the issue of your absence in class this evening. I'm afraid I'm a bit of an old-school professor."

Yes, he was. And his hand was right back on that ruler again. Her lips suddenly seemed so dry. She had to lick them, the way she would likely end up licking him. "I'm willing to do whatever it takes to make up for my mistake, Professor."

She sat down in front of him and wished she'd been able to put on a little skirt and white shirt and put her hair up in pigtails. The full Britney. But she could make the fantasy happen with what she had to work with. She unbuttoned the first button of her blouse, and then a second and a third until she was sure he could see the tops of her breasts.

"Has it gotten hot in here, Ms. Lyndon?"

Time for some truth. "I'd prefer Ms. Slaten, Professor. I'm afraid when I signed up for your class I was still going by my married name."

Something happened to Flynn. He went still and just for a moment she thought he was going to break character. "Slaten, is it?"

"I've always hated the name so when I had the chance to change it, I did." She'd actually changed it because there was a clause in Frankie's company bylaws that stated family stock could only be held by wives who legally changed their names.

Yeah, they'd taken over Frankie's company, too, and he'd already changed that backward rule.

He paused for a moment and then there was something soft about his tone. "Ms. Slaten. I don't mind it. It suits you."

He wouldn't say that if he knew her father. "How can I fix things, Professor? And yes, it's rather hot in here."

"Then you should take off that shirt. I wouldn't want you uncomfortable."

She eased out of her shirt. It wasn't at all hot in her apartment. In fact, it was a little cool, and she shivered as the air hit her skin, her nipples puckering.

"That undergarment looks uncomfortable," Flynn said in a deep voice. "I'm afraid I'll have to insist you take that off as well. This isn't your first infraction. I've been indulgent, but now I have to move past notes and verbal warnings."

She undid her bra and folded it with her top. "I'm willing to do anything to make up the class, Professor."

He reached over and opened a box. "I'm a strict disciplinarian. I'm going to give you something to think about. Do you know what these are?"

He pulled out two little clamps.

She gasped and something twisted deep inside her body, an anticipation of pleasure. "Those are clamps, Sir."

"Yes, very good. Do you know where I'm going to place them?"

She had a good idea and it made her skin tingle. "On my nipples."

"I'm going to need you to get them ready. Proper preparation is required for this course. You haven't shown me that yet. Show me you can prepare yourself, Ms. Slaten."

Nipple clamps. She'd read about them in Bridget's books and they'd been some of the toys shown to them during demos. She'd watched the other subs in her group play around with them. Even Regina, who was so tough, had laughed and played with Jolie and Lucy. Only she had sat back.

Had she ever simply played around? Did there always have to be purpose to what she did?

She cupped her breasts, letting herself feel the weight of them in her hands.

"Tell me how they feel to you. Consider it an oral essay. Tell me what you like about touching your breasts." Flynn commanded her with a dark tone. Her Dom had relaxed. It was easy to see by the set of his shoulders, how he sat back in the chair as though certain he would get an excellent show.

Had he been nervous? Had he worried she would reject him or not want this type of play?

She took a deep breath and let the moment wash over her. "I like how smooth my skin is. It's cool to the touch, but that's only on the outside."

"And inside?"

"I'm warming up nicely, Sir." That was an understatement. She'd never considered her own body before. Not like this. She'd bemoaned it, cursed it. Sometimes she'd felt some accomplishment in it. But she'd never simply run her hands over it and reveled in how it reacted, how well it had been made. "I like the contrast of smooth skin and hard nipples. Though they're not truly hard. They're ready."

"Oh, I doubt that," he replied. "I think I need to see this up close. You know professors are curious animals. We need to study a subject carefully. Come here, Ms. Slaten. Let me take a look and see if you're truly ready for the beginning of my lesson."

She stood, still in her heels. Her feet ached, but she wasn't getting out of them. Flynn liked her in heels. He would sometimes keep her in heels and nothing else. She moved around the table and wondered briefly if she would ever be able to sit at it again without see Flynn. He remained seated, looking like a decadent gift.

Amy offered her breasts up. "See. They're perfectly rigid. All you have to do is ease the clamps on."

They would be little jewels on her nipples, making her breasts a gift to her Master.

It was getting harder and harder to think of him as anything less. He was the man who'd taught her she could let go, be safe with him. He was the one who'd truly taken her out of her former mindset and allowed her to savor what it meant to be one with a man.

He sat up and suddenly his hands were on her hips, right at the waistband of her skirt. "I don't know. They look like they need a little something more. Sometimes it's better to show than tell. I'm going to need you to clasp your hands behind your back."

She did as he asked, the motion forcing her breasts out, thrusting them toward him. "Like that?"

"Exactly like that." He reached up and let a single fingertip trace the areola of her right breast. "You have lovely breasts."

"I've always worried they were too small," she admitted. Holding her hands behind her back made her vulnerable to him, on display for all to see, though there was only Flynn. In the club if he did this, she would be visible to everyone, but she rather thought it would be the same. Only he would matter. "I'm afraid my sister got the big boobs in our family."

He rolled the nipple between his thumb and forefinger. "These are beautifully formed and you're right. The skin is perfect. I would give these an A plus, but you're not ready for what I have to give you. Not quite yet."

He leaned forward and licked her right nipple, sending a wave of sensation through her body. He drew her in, between his legs. His big arms wrapped around her and he set his mouth on her nipple. He sucked and licked and laved it with affection. She had to force herself to remain still or she would have squirmed against him.

Gingerly, he slipped the clamp on, the little teeth biting into her sensitized nipple. That's what the bastard had been doing. He'd licked and sucked her so she would feel every one of those nasty teeth. She gasped as the jewel attached weighed her nipple down.

There was pain and yet it made her wet and ready. She couldn't think of anything beyond the fact that he was holding her tight, capturing her left nipple with those sensual lips of his and bringing it to life.

He engaged the second clamp and sat back, looking at his handiwork. "Yes, I believe that will do, Ms. Slaten. Now I'm going to have to ask you a very important question. Do you remember the rules of this class?"

She knew he wasn't talking about the class. He was talking about their rules. Her breasts were so sensitive. Moving even the slightest bit made the jewels on the clamps tug at her nipples as though Flynn's mouth and teeth were still there, still torturing her in the sweetest way. "Yes, Sir. I remember."

"Excellent. What are you supposed to do on days when we play?"

She saw the trap the minute the question came out of his mouth and she realized she was in some serious trouble. Her spanking might turn into a non-erotic one. Damn. Could she get out of this?

His eyes narrowed. "Don't even try. I had a rule. I suspect you didn't follow it. You're quite obedient, pet. You've never disobeyed me in this. Not once when I've checked have I found you slacking."

Panties. She wasn't allowed to wear them at all on days when they were going to play. He'd told her it was all about anticipation. He wanted her to think about him all day, so she got to go commando on the days they went to class.

Logic would state that since she'd texted him at the last minute to let him know she couldn't make the class that she shouldn't be wearing underwear.

Except she was because she'd known all along she wasn't going to be able to make that class. She'd just put off telling him until she'd known she was going to walk into the meeting and turn off her phone.

When he would pick her up for class, she would get into the seat beside him and he would request that she spread her legs. His big hand would move up her thigh and he would tease her pussy for a moment, starting the evening off right and letting her settle into the safety of subspace.

He was going to be so pissed.

"Ms. Slaten, you know the rules of this class. I think you should show me that you are wearing the proper uniform. Otherwise, I might decide that your skipping my lecture this evening wasn't an accident but rather something you planned and failed to discuss with me."

"That would be bad, right?"

He picked up that nasty-looking ruler. "That would be very bad, pet. Pull up the skirt right now."

Damn, it was the first time she was actually in trouble with him and it really did something for her. It was all a game and she could end it very quickly. The rules had been agreed to for their mutual pleasure and satisfaction, and this had been agreed to for the very same reasons. Because he would like spanking her and she would enjoy being spanked.

Hard.

Fuck, she needed it hard tonight. It didn't matter if it made her weird. It would make her Amy and she so needed to be herself for a few hours. Not the CEO. Not the rebel daughter or the woman who was going to save jobs. Not Frankie's best friend.

Her. This was who she was in the center of herself. This was her sexual self, the one that came out when she tossed aside all notions of respectability and got down to what she wanted.

She wanted Flynn and she wanted that ruler on her ass.

She pulled up her skirt, the fabric gliding along her skin until her undies showed.

His frown deepened. "Why?"

She owed him honesty. "I'd already missed one class. I knew you would be disappointed in me and I enjoy our calls during the day. You picked me up for lunch and I didn't want it spoiled. I wanted my time with you."

He stared down at her for a moment, taking her chin in one hand and looking her straight in the eyes. "I want my time with you too, pet. And so you'll understand me, I will never punish you for working hard. Never. I won't withdraw affection or sulk like a child. I would have come and picked you up for lunch whether or not you had joined me tonight. I'm beginning to believe you haven't been able to count on the men in your life very often. I'm different."

He would have to be compared to every other man in her life. She loved Frankie, but he couldn't be this for her. "I'll remember."

"I intend to make you remember, pet. Bend over my desk, palms flat, and spread those legs."

"Shouldn't I…" She was going to ask if he wanted her to take off the undies first.

She didn't get the chance. He let go of her chin and reached out, tugging on the clamp. Fire raced through her, the pain making her gasp and then turning into heat deep inside.

"You should do exactly as I say and not question any more tonight, Ms. Slaten. Or you'll find your grade plummets. Am I understood?"

She turned and placed her palms flat on the table, spread her legs wide. The only reason she could do that was the fact that her skirt was currently around her waist. It was awkward, but she tossed out that line of thought. Flynn wouldn't care that it was odd. He would only care that he had access to her backside and that this position he'd placed her in caused gravity to work on the clamps. They pulled at her nipples, making her breasts feel heavy and full.

"Yes, Professor."

He leaned down and suddenly sounded like Flynn again, the sweet wonderful Flynn who rubbed her feet at night and cuddled on his couch with her. "Except for your safe word. You know that, right? You can always say that."

She had to smile. "I do."

"Cool. Sorry, this is my first time role-playing. And I meant what I said about being there for you. Don't ever think I won't because I'm disappointed." He kissed her cheek, a soft buss on her skin. "Back to stern professor mode."

She had played before and breaking character wasn't acceptable with some of her previous lovers. But her heart did a weird flip as she realized he would do anything to make sure she understood how he intended to care about her.

She was falling in love with him. She might already be there.

She would have to tell him about her father, but she wasn't going to let him go. She was going to fight for this man. He was worth everything she had.

God, she might have found the one thing she wanted more than the company.

"You don't have to take off the panties because I'm going to deal with them. I'm going to ensure this particular pair never comes back to my classroom again."

She felt something cold slide against her flesh and then the sound of her undies being cut off, first one side and then the other.

"You're prepared, Professor." The damn man had known what she'd done all along. Or at least he'd strongly suspected.

He pulled the undies from her and she felt the caress of air on her skin.

"I'm always prepared and I think you'll find I've gotten to know you rather well. I know how you work. You text when you want to avoid confrontation. I won't allow you to avoid me. I'm going to need a count, Ms. Slaten."

There was a nice whoosh and then she heard the crack of the ruler against her backside. Her breath fled and the pain bloomed, but she could handle it. "One."

The ruler struck again.

"Two."

And again.

"Three."

This time he struck the under curve of her ass, making her shake and the clamps on her nipples shimmy in delicious time to the whacks. Her breasts bounced, the clamps biting into her nipples.

She counted it out as he continued to spank her. Every slap of the ruler burned and sizzled. Every time the ruler struck, a spark of electricity shot through her. Tears dripped from her eyes. She could cry here. She could let it out.

All the stress leached from her system as he worked her over. She clung to the desk, letting him take her further and further. She could hear her voice, counting out each stroke, but it seemed distant. She was lost in her own body, in her connection to him.

The tears came but not like they had that first night. She didn't need it as much now. She needed something different from him and as he continued, every stroke of the ruler took her to another level. The pain mixed with the pleasure to create something new, something dark and seemingly forbidden, something she'd come to crave.

"Forty," she said with a shiver.

This time his hand came out, cupping her cheek and stroking over her heated flesh.

"Very nice. You handled that assignment quite well." Her horny professor's voice was anything but even.

"Do I get an A?" She wasn't sure how much further she could take this. She'd always adored role-play, but she kind of wanted Flynn now.

He hauled her up and turned her around, his hair escaping from the tight queue he'd placed it in. "I'll give you anything you want but I don't think I can keep this up. I need you, Amy."

There he was. There was her Flynn. He could be so dominant and yet he made himself vulnerable to her. He was perfect because they could play and play but when it got real he was right there with her.

"I'm crazy about you, Flynn. I think…" She wasn't ready to say it yet.

His lips curled up slightly and his eyes lit. "I think, too. I think we think about the same damn things. Come here. I fucking need you in my life. Don't ever put me off with a text again. Call me. Tell me what you need and I'll give it to you."

She'd never heard those words from a man before. Never believed them.

One hand cupped the back of her neck and he pulled her in for a hungry kiss. She was so aware of her own body. He was still dressed, the tweed of his jacket scratching against her.

He pulled away and without a word, picked her up and set her on the table. "Let me get these off you. Hold on. It's going to hurt a little, but I'll make it all better for you, pet. I waited all fucking day to be here with you. I'll make everything better. Lean back for me."

She did as he asked, offering her clamped breasts up to him. Offering everything up to him.

He undid the first clamp and she nearly screamed as the blood rushed back into her nipple. He was there, soothing her with his lips and tongue. Though she knew he was eager, he didn't rush through the process. He took his time, ensuring she was all right. That was the heart of who he was. She bit back against the pain of her second nipple being freed because she knew Flynn would make it better. Even as he laved his affection on her tortured nipples, his free hand played in her pussy.

The spanking had gotten her hot and wet. She didn't need anything but his cock and yet he stayed at her breasts for a moment, kissing and sucking gently until she thought she would explode with wanting.

He moved back and shoved at his slacks. He didn't bother with the shirt or the jacket, simply shoved down his pants and boxers, freeing his cock. He proved just how prepared he'd been. Next to where he'd lain the ruler was a condom. With a quick tear and an expert hand, he prepped it and rolled it on before lining himself up.

"This has been your lesson in role-playing," he said with a grin. He looked at her like she was the most precious thing in the world. "Please tell Wade I properly instructed you on the finer points of the subject."

She wasn't sure how much true role-playing they'd done, but she loved him for trying. He was even sexier when he couldn't keep in character because he had to have her, needed to be close to her. "I'll be sure to let him know that your methods work wonders, Professor."

He pressed in, filling her up. He was so big and hard inside her. She spread herself wide and then wrapped her legs around him. She could feel him on every inch of her skin. Her backside ached against the desk, her nipples still tender, but it was all part of the play. She wanted more of it, more of him.

She groaned as he thrust inside her and pulled back out. He leaned over to kiss her, tongue thrusting in time to his cock.

How could he do this to her? She'd never reacted to a man like she did Flynn. Already she could feel herself on the shimmering edge.

"Do you have any idea how good you make me feel?" Flynn whispered against her lips. His arms went to her tender backside, holding her tight.

She groaned at the sensation. So much sensation. He rocked into her, hitting her clit with his pelvis, rubbing and moving in a way that had her screaming out his name in no time.

He kept it up until finally his back bowed and he tightened his arms around her, keeping her close to him. His cock plunged in one last time and he was spent.

"That was a perfect lesson," she said with a smile as she lay back on the desk and tried to catch her breath. Her body pulsed with the sweet exertion.

He was so gorgeous as he stared down at her. His hand came out, touching her chest right in between her breasts. "It's not over. I've got a lot to teach you. First tell me something, pet. Was it a hard day?"

It had been awful. There were those tears again, but they were somehow sweet because he was here with her. "Yes."

"Then I'll get myself cleaned up and I'm going to get you out of those gorgeous heels and rub your feet while you eat the pizza I ordered. It's ham and pineapple. Just like you like it. I'll make it better for you, Amy…Slaten. I like Slaten better."

He stepped away and she could hear him moving to her bathroom.

She'd never cared for the name at all, but somehow it sounded right when he said it.

Amy let the peace of the moment settle over her and knew that no matter what happened in the morning she was going to be all right.

For the first time in her life she felt comfortable in her own skin.

Chapter Seven

Flynn put the glass of wine in front of Amy with a deep sense of satisfaction. He hadn't been an awful professor. Oh, he'd broken character more than once, but they would get better at it. She seemed to respond well. So very well. "You liked the pizza, pet?"

She smiled up at him, her skin still flush from all the nasty things he'd done to her. He hadn't allowed her to get dressed again. When she got cold, he'd wrapped her in a blanket after ensuring the gorgeous flesh of her ass was merely pink and not likely to welt. "It was delicious and so much better than anything I was planning."

He sank down beside her. "What were you planning? Because from what I can tell you have very little food in this place."

She groaned and settled herself against him. "I've done nothing except work and go over to your place for the last few weeks. No time for grocery shopping. I'm afraid you've been my main source of nutrition."

He didn't mind that at all. He liked providing for her. He also liked that they were finally talking. She'd been stressed for weeks but when he asked about it she deflected. He ran a hand over her hair. "Work is rough?"

"My company is in some trouble and it's been one thing after another." She was quiet for a moment and then seemed to come to a decision. "Honestly, it's in a lot of trouble. Everything's coming to a head and I've been putting out one fire after another."

Slaten Industries was her company and she'd admitted that was her true last name and given him a decent explanation for why she'd changed it. Nothing in her manner had told him she was lying to him or hiding anything. She'd simply been admitting something that she hadn't thought was important. She hadn't liked hearing a name she didn't consider her own and that was when she'd explained it to him.

She had no idea who he was and she wasn't some corporate spy. She was his sweet, sexy, hard-working girl.

Who would have fucking guessed his perfect woman would turn out to be the head of Slaten Industries? His father had to be having a good laugh. He didn't even consider that his father would be angry. He wouldn't. He might have hated George Slaten, but he would have loved Amy.

Now he had to figure out how to explain to her that his last name wasn't Flynn. That in and of itself wasn't the problem. The problem was that his last name was Adler, and he thought that might mean something to her.

She might be innocent in all this but he wasn't. Still, if he explained maybe it wouldn't be too bad. He could massage it, maybe bring it up in conversation and then act like it was all one big surprise.

It kind of had been.

"Putting out fires doesn't sound good."

She groaned and cuddled against him. "Awful."

"You don't talk about work much. I'm not sure if that's because you don't enjoy your work or if it's sensitive."

"Sensitive?"

"Like my work. I keep everything private because of the nature of the code I'm writing." This could be a good talk. And he couldn't think of a better way to broach the subject than with her naked and sated in his arms.

"That's right. You're in R&D. Is that why you freaked out on me that morning?"

He chuckled. It was easy now because he could look back and see how completely paranoid he'd been. Amy wasn't great with a computer. His girl wouldn't know how to steal his code, much less even want to. Something else had happened to put those scratches on that system. He would figure it out, but he knew it couldn't have been her. "I'd been dealing with some rival firms trying to get hold of it. It's worth a lot of money, but I overreacted. It will never happen again. You can use my computer anytime you like."

"I can play solitaire?" She yawned, putting her hand over her mouth.

He kissed her forehead. "I'll get you your own password and everything."

He trusted her. Now that she'd told him her real name, he realized how foolish he'd been. Still, he wouldn't change a thing. He was perfectly happy where he was.

"You might not after I tell you what I have to tell you." She turned and twisted until she was facing him, gathering the blanket around her.

His stomach threatened to drop. "What's that?"

"I don't talk about work because it's not pleasant for me," she began. It was easy to see the tension was back in her shoulders. They were practically up around her ears. "My family owns the majority of the stock in our company and they're not exactly the nicest people in the world. I'm fairly certain my father is one of Satan's minions. He's truly vile. My mom spends most of her time with her Chardonnay, but I probably would too if I was married to my father."

"You work with your dad?" Mitch had told him a little, but not much. Adam had filled in some lines, but he still had some questions.

She bit her bottom lip and was quiet for a moment, as though trying to figure out how much to tell him. "I kind of ousted him and took over his role as CEO."

"You got him voted out?"

"Sort of. I might have had a private investigator follow him around until he broke his own morality clause. I might have had the whole thing taped and I might have shown it as the video reel at my wedding. Which was also for business purposes. When I married Frankie, he got stock and a voting share at Slaten and I got one in his family's company when I took his name. We took down our parents in a two-week period."

She was mean. Why did that get him hot? "Your father was that bad?"

"He was planning on selling the company and using the sale as a way of screwing the employees not only out of their jobs but out of their pensions. When my grandfather ran Slaten, he offered pensions, and we've still got about fifty older employees who stand to come into theirs in the next few years, and a hundred or so retired employees who would have found themselves totally screwed over. My father made some shady legal maneuvers a few years back. While they could have fought it, he would have money-whipped them. I had a lawyer attached to McKay-Taggart look at everything before I took over and he pointed out all the ways my father intended to screw our employees. I grew up with a bunch of them. I worked at Slaten every summer and they took care of me. I couldn't let that happen. I couldn't let him do that to the company my grandfather worked so hard to build."

"Mitch?"

She nodded. "Yeah. The lawyer's name was Mitch Bradford. I wanted to hire him full time, but apparently I can't afford him."

"He's my brother." Finally a bit of the truth. It felt good.

"Will told me," she admitted. "He said you and Mitch are half brothers and you haven't known each other very long."

That was good old Mitch. He likely hadn't said much more about him to Will. The man was Mitch's best friend, but Mitch wasn't a talker. They played a lot of pick-up basketball and regularly watched football games and barbecued, but Mitch had likely never talked about Glendale with his friend. He wondered if Mitch would consider it attorney-client privilege since Mitch served as Flynn's personal attorney.

"I have a younger brother too. I think I've mentioned him. Chase."

"I like how you smile when you talk about him," she said quietly.

"He's a good kid. My stepmom, Chase's biological mother, died of breast cancer and then Dad got sick. My own precious mother couldn't be bothered with us. I kind of raised him the last couple of years and he's turned out great." Once he'd gotten Chase away from the bad influence of bullies and kids who thought drugs were better than therapy.

Her expression soured. "Another reason you might not want to see me again after tonight. I didn't think about the fact that you had a younger brother. He probably looks up to you."

"I hope so. Amy, come out and say what you need to say." He was getting anxious. What was she getting at?

"My father knows about Sanctum and he's going to use it to tell the board I'm immoral and therefore incapable of being CEO."

He had to laugh. "Morality has zero to do with being a great CEO. I can promise you that or half of the CEOs on the Fortune 500 would be out of a job."

She shook her head. "He'll take it to the press and I'll become the female CEO who likes to get spanked. And before you laugh again, it's different for a woman in power and you know it."

He sobered a bit. "I do, but I think you're overreacting. You're allowed to have a private life."

"Not in my family I'm not. You need to think about this. He's suing me already. I didn't think about the fact that you could end up getting dragged into it. What will your brothers think? They could ask you all kinds of questions. The press could get hold of the story. You could lose your job. God, I don't even want to think about what could happen if Glendale gets wind of it. They'll use it against all of us."

He stilled. "Glendale."

Her jaw went stubborn. "It's a rival firm. Normally I would tell you not to worry about them. I thought when John Sr. died and I took over Slaten that it would be over, but his son turned out to be just as bad as he ever was. He hates me."

"I'm sure he doesn't." He didn't want her to think that for a second.

She shook her head. "Trust me. The man is horrible. He might be worse than his father. His CEO informed me yesterday that he's planning on siccing the FTC on me if I don't back away from a company he wants. He says he's got an informant who's willing to testify I've been manipulating stock. I don't put it past that man to invent evidence."

"What?" He hadn't authorized anything like that. What the hell was Curt doing?

"It won't work. I'm still meeting with them. Tomorrow, in fact. I need that company. If I can't get them to sign on, I'm probably not going to have a job next week. So I need you to seriously think about continuing on with me. I know I should quit the training program."

That wasn't happening. He needed to figure out what the hell his CEO was doing and correct it. If that meant giving Amy and Slaten the Clannahan deal, then that was what he would do.

He would do it. Huh. It was easy when he didn't think about it, when he allowed his instinct to rule. He knew exactly what he would do. He would give her what she needed without question.

Maybe then she would see he wasn't as bad as his father.

"Absolutely not." He put a little Dom tone behind that command.

"I can't risk putting Sanctum in a bad position." She shook her head as though making up her mind. "Everyone has been so kind to me. Maybe when it all shakes out in a few months I can try again."

He reached out and dragged her back to his side of the couch, hauling her close. "You are not quitting anything and if you think for a second this scares me off, you're wrong. It makes me mad, but it doesn't make me want to bail on you."

It made him want to protect her. Unfortunately, it looked like she needed protection from his own company.

She wrapped her arms around him and settled her head on his chest. "What will your family think? You have to consider them, Flynn. And your employer."

"My family is all pretty much at Sanctum with the exception of Chase and my nephew. And Chase knows I'm a pervert. He's always known." He smoothed her hair back. "As for work, I'd like to see them try to get rid of me. This is nothing I want you to worry about. You have a big meeting tomorrow. I want you to rest. Don't worry about anything. It's going to be fine, pet. You do your best and the rest is going to work itself out."

"I don't know about that," she murmured.

He soothed a hand down her back. The blanket had come off but she seemed fine. He let his hand run the length of her spine. "It will. Can I stay here with you tonight?"

She hugged him. "I would love that."

He was getting addicted to waking up with her, sleeping with her, doing everything with her. "I don't want to be anywhere else. And I'll be there for you tomorrow no matter what happens in that meeting. I'll be there and we can sit down and talk."

"Or you can help me pack up my office."

He actually liked that she was being so open with him. She usually pulled an invisible cloak around herself and shut down when it came to work. But she could tell him anything. He could hold her and let her cry or be afraid or angry.

"I don't think it's going to come to that." He would make sure of it.

She was quiet for a moment and after a while he noticed her breathing had settled into a rhythm. She'd fallen asleep right on his chest, her arms around him.

God, she was beautiful. The thought that he could lose her was an actual ache in his body. She was the one. He hadn't thought there really was a one, but Amy Slaten proved him wrong.

He eased up, shifting her in his arms. Her eyes opened.

"Go back to sleep," he said gently as he stood up.

"You make me feel almost small when you pick me up," she said with a yawn.

"You are small compared to me." He moved back to her bedroom.

He settled her into her too small for the both of them bed. It was probably a queen, but he took up a lot of space. He wanted her at his place, in his bed and in his shower and humming in his kitchen while she made breakfast.

Theirs. It could be theirs. He would let her do whatever she wanted with it as long as she stayed with him.

He kissed her on the forehead, but she was already back to sleep.

He had a call to make. Flynn strode back into the living room so he wouldn't disturb her. Luckily, the man he was calling was on West Coast time. He also took his time answering. Curt picked up on the fourth ring.

"Hey, Flynn, how's it going out in Dallas?" In the background it sounded like Curt was at a party of some kind, or perhaps he'd walked out of a crowded restaurant.

He wasn't going to waste time on small talk. "I need you to tell Clannahan that the deal's off."

It sounded as though Curt had moved farther from the noise. "Excuse me?"

He was springing this on him without any warning. Flynn tried to slow down. "I've changed my mind about the Clannahan deal. I don't want the company anymore. We haven't signed anything yet so it should be easy to call off the deal."

"Call off the deal? I'm not calling off the deal, Flynn. We need that company as a base to distribute the software around the world."

"The German company would work just as well." They'd looked at several international firms that could handle their distribution.

"The German company is twice the outlay of cash," Curt pointed out.

"Doesn't matter. We've got plenty and we'll have more when the code's done."

There was a pause over the line. "Does this have anything to do with the fact that you're sleeping with Amy Slaten?"

"What?" He hadn't expected to hear those words.

"You're sleeping with the enemy, Flynn. Did you think I wouldn't hear about that?"

"I'm wondering how the fuck you know about that."

"I know because I keep track of the major players in my organization. You're too important to Glendale to not keep watch over. You do understand that she's playing you, right? You can't possibly be that naïve."

He didn't like the idea that someone had been spying on him. "Do you have a private eye watching me or something?"

"I don't need one. I send enough people out to Dallas to get your signature on things that they can tell me who you're sleeping with. You take her out all the time and she's gotten very cozy in your building. You've let her into your place? Where you keep the code? I thought you were smarter that that."

"She doesn't care about the code. She has no idea who the hell I am."

A huff came over the line. "Don't be ridiculous. Look, I've been indulgent so far, but I'm certainly not going to let a company that can do us good get away because your girlfriend gave you a blow job or something."

Anger welled inside him. No one got to talk about her like she was some kind of easy lay. No one. "You're fired."

"You can't fire me," he replied. "Not like that and I can assure you I have more sway over your board than you do right now. You're the playboy who couldn't care less about this company or managing it properly. You want to be left alone with your code. Well, this is you getting left alone with your code. You didn't want the responsibility, this is what that looks like, Flynn. And let me tell you something. Your girl isn't as squeaky clean as she looks. The way her father tells it, she's the one behind all the recent spying. Hell, she's apparently been playing fast and loose with her stock."

So that's where it had come from. At one point, Flynn might have stopped to investigate, but he didn't need to do that anymore. "Her father is using you. He's trying to get his job back."

"From what I can tell he probably deserves it. Hell, I don't know. I don't care. After they lose Clannahan and I explain to several big business reporters exactly what that means, their stock is going to tank and I'll swoop in, buy it for a song, and break the fucker into pieces. Your father would be proud. He always hated Slaten."

"You'll do nothing of the kind." It would kill her to lose that company. She'd sacrificed for it, worked her ass off. "Don't even try to finalize that deal. I'll block you."

"You can certainly try, but you'll find unless the board drops me, you're in a bind for the terms of my contract. Like I said, I've been indulgent, but now I'm going to do my job and that's making the absolute most money I can possibly make whatever it takes. I've got a party to get back to. Why don't you go and write some more code, Flynn? Leave the business to the men who know how to get it done."

The line went dead and Flynn thought about getting on the first plane to California, finding that fucker and throttling him.

"Hey, are you okay?"

He turned and Amy was standing in the doorway, a sheet wrapped around her. She looked sleepy and the slightest bit worried.

She had the meeting of a lifetime in the morning and there was nothing he could do tonight to fix things for her. Mitch would already be asleep and he turned off the phones after ten so nothing would wake up the baby.

He moved to her. The morning would be soon enough to find a way out.

"I'm fine, pet. Let's get to bed." He kissed her, promising himself that no matter what, he would find a way to save her company.

Then he would find a way to get her to forgive him.

Chapter Eight

Amy took a deep breath and stepped into the room. It was show time and there was nothing else to do but lay her cards on the table and hope they played out.

Padraig Clannahan and his older brother, Seamus, were dressed in perfectly pressed suits, both looking like men ready to do business. Their suits were pristine, but their demeanors were much more casual. Neither had even glanced at the proposal she'd given them. They were more interested in the tea she'd served. She knew they weren't exactly taking her seriously, but she meant to change that.

She shook their hands as the conference room filled up. Her lawyer was present along with a few of her senior team members. And the newest team member, the one whose office was mostly for show, but he would definitely be collecting a paycheck if this worked out. She would owe him big time.

"Gentlemen, I hope your flight was satisfactory."

Padraig was in his fifties, a silver fox of a man. He gave her a winning smile as he sat back. "It was perfectly lovely, Ms. Slaten. I thank you for taking such good care of two old Irishmen."

Seamus shook his head. "Speak for yerself, brother. I'm not old at all, darlin'. But I did very much appreciate the excellent whiskey, and the coddle was better than me mum used to make. Very surprised to have that served. Airplane food is usually soggy pasta or overdone beef."

Coddle was a traditional Irish pork dish and Sean Taggart had taught the chef Slaten used on their corporate jet how to make it just right. It was the Clannahan brothers' favorite dish. A fact she'd learned because she'd done her homework. She'd wanted those Irishmen in a good mood when they got off the plane.

"I thought a bit of home would make you feel comfortable."

"It was much appreciated." Padraig sent his brother a stare. "The other ones thought we would like all those green things and that uncooked fish."

Ah, California cuisine. It looked like Glendale had tried to wow them with sushi and kale. She'd learned a long time ago that proving she could cater to a client's likes was far better than shoving her own at them.

Seamus didn't take the bait. He turned Amy's way. "As much as we love good food, we need to talk about business. You've proven yourself to be a damn fine hostess, and I appreciate that, but you have to know we've talked to Glendale."

"Of course." She was pleased her voice sounded so even, professional. She'd woken up and Flynn had coffee waiting for her. He'd kissed her senseless and promised her everything would be okay.

She wasn't sure she believed him, but he'd given her strength.

He would be there when she called him this evening. He'd dropped her off so she could go over her notes. She was going to call him and he would pour her a glass of wine and she would cuddle with him. Win or lose at least she would have Flynn.

"I expected that Glendale would contact you. We often have the same interests." And they liked to take anything Slaten wanted.

"They have a software product they want us to distribute," Padraig explained. "From a very up and coming young coder. They've convinced us the software he's developing is going to be very big."

She was sure they did. "Yes, I assume they want to give you a small piece of the pie."

He nodded. "We've talked about a percentage."

It would be small. Glendale was arrogant. It was a function of their size. They rarely had to think about truly sending anything but cash down the pipeline. The truth was a small but powerful family company like Clannahan sometimes had different priorities. Sometimes money wasn't as big a factor as it seemed to be.

She'd researched them enough to know that was true for the two men sitting across from her.

"How many Irish workers are they willing to employ?"

Seamus frowned. "They only want us to handle distribution."

"That's what I suspected. Have they offered to buy you out? Are you aware the last three companies they purchased were absorbed by Glendale and within a few years they ceased to exist as entities?"

Padraig put up a hand to stop her. "We talked about that. They've given us their word that we'll still function on our own."

"Yes, I'm sure they'll promise you that, but they won't put it in writing."

Seamus's eyes narrowed. "You will?"

"I'm not trying to buy your company, Mr. Clannahan. That's what Glendale will end up doing no matter what they choose to call it. I'm offering a partnership. We've got products and services we need to move into the European market. You give us everything we need to work in that part of the world and we can do the same here for you in the States. I can not offer you the kind of money Glendale can upfront. If what you want to do is sell your company to a massive American conglomerate, take the cash and retire, then we should end this meeting now."

"I'm not ready to retire and I've got two boys who want to carry on for us," Padraig said, his face turning a shade of red.

Yes, she had him now. "But if you want a partnership that could benefit both of us, then take a look at my proposal. The money isn't upfront and it isn't guaranteed. But if we work hard there's a pot of gold at the end of this rainbow and I am going to make sure you get a nice portion of it. First though, I'm going to need for you to hire at least five more full-time positions on your end and Slaten will pay those salaries."

She saw the moment the gentlemen decided to take her seriously. The brothers shared a long look and then moved to open the proposal books in front of them.

The Clannahans believed in their community. They'd raised themselves up from poverty, become wildly successful, and yet they still lived in the town they'd grown up in. They were the patrons of their people, generating jobs and putting local kids through college.

They believed in their town, their country, and that was what Glendale didn't understand.

"Five full-time positions?" Seamus put on his reading glasses. "Is that what you said?"

"Yes, five in the beginning, but if my projections are correct, we'll double that in the next three years. I've also brought in my security liaison to explain how we're going to upgrade your cyber security."

"We've had problems with that," Padraig said with a sigh. "I'll admit I don't know a lot about it and we've been lax. I don't understand all those young people they bring in to do the jobs. It's all gibberish to me."

They were on the hook. She could feel it. Now it was time for her ace in the hole to reel them in. She smiled and turned to the stunning man on her left. "Let me introduce our VP of security, Liam O'Donnell."

Liam O'Donnell was a gorgeous dark-haired man in his mid thirties. He could have been a model or an actor, but he'd joined the Irish military and then had done work for G2, Irish intelligence, and now was a senior member of the McKay-Taggart team. He was also her new VP of security. It was a job he already did, as McKay-Taggart handled her security and he was her liaison, but now he had an office and everything. He wouldn't be leaving his primary job, but he would be handling Clannahan and taking a nice-sized cut of the profits on the backend as his salary.

She had to hope it worked.

"O'Donnell?" Padraig asked.

"Straight out of Dublin," O'Donnell said, holding his hand out.

Padraig shook his hand and then Seamus greeted him. When they sat back down, both men were serious.

"I think we should talk," Padraig said.

"Definitely," Seamus agreed. "I want to hear about this plan."

"If you'll turn to page fifteen, I think I can explain everything to you in plain language," O'Donnell said, beginning his portion of the meeting.

Plain language? He was speaking their language.

Amy sat back, comfortable that she was going to win this round.

Three hours later, she grinned up at O'Donnell. "Li, you're worth every penny I'm going to spend on you over the next few years."

He winked her way. "I'll make sure of it. I think I'll enjoy this side job. I've avoided going back to Ireland for years. Now all I can think of is showing my wife and son how beautiful my country is. Unfortunately, my McKay-Taggart work never takes me back there. This will be good for me."

"Ian Taggart isn't worried I'll lure you to the corporate side?" She'd offered him a full-time position. She still kind of hoped he would take it some day. He would be an incredible asset.

"Never," he swore with a smile. "I'm more than happy to do this on a limited basis, but my heart's in McKay-Taggart. Oh, I'll eventually move more into management over there and let the youngsters take the bullets, but I love solving a good mystery. Keeps a man on his feet. Still, you call me when you have any trouble at all. Erin or I will come running. Well, Erin doesn't run a lot these days. She kind of waddles but I don't ever mention that to her because she still enjoys shooting people. Pregnancy hasn't taken the violence out of that girl one bit, I tell you."

Erin Argent was in the same Lamaze class as her sister. She was also Liam's partner at MT. The pretty redhead was intimidating even at eight months pregnant.

"I'll let you know and I'll make sure everything is first class for you and Aidan and Avery when you go out to Clannahan next month." She still couldn't believe it was all done. She had their signatures on the contract and Glendale could bite her ass.

She was partying tonight after class. She was taking her Dom out for drinks and dancing and then some kinky sex back at his place. Definitely his place, though, since she'd discovered he was a mattress hog and required the California king to be comfy.

All around her the news was getting out. Employees were smiling and the relief was almost palpable.

Liam walked with her toward her office. "They're all thrilled with you, Amy. Don't be too surprised if they start uncorking the champagne I might have brought."

She couldn't help but smile. The man was an optimist. "You

brought a case of champagne?"

"Always. If we hadn't won them over, it would have been conciliatory champagne. As it is, now it's celebratory."

Sure enough she heard a cork pop and someone turned on the music. They wouldn't be getting much done this afternoon, but she was all right with that. They deserved a party. It had been a stressful year and they could relax.

Maybe she would call Flynn and have him come over. She wanted him to meet her friends and coworkers. For weeks she'd kept him out of this part of her life, but now she wanted him here with her.

"Perhaps you and your new man can join us when we go. I think it would be good for everyone involved if you came out for that first tour with me," Liam was saying as they rounded the corner to her office. "I hear you've made a real connection with Mitch's younger brother."

And there was the stupid smile she couldn't seem to get rid of. "Flynn is incredible. I don't know what mojo Kai works but he did an amazing job when he put the two of us together. But I have to start trying to call him John. I can't keep calling my boyfriend by his last name."

"I thought Flynn was his middle name."

"No. It's John Flynn. He doesn't have the same last name as Mitch because Mitch's mother wasn't married to their dad. He says everyone calls him Flynn because he likes his last name more than John. I'll be honest I like Flynn more than John. John makes me think of John Adler and I mostly want to strangle that guy." She gave her assistant a wave. "Hey, Val. I thought you would be out on the floor partying. We got it. Don't look so glum."

Val was the only person in the office who wasn't wearing a goofy grin. "You have a delivery in your office. It's from your father."

Now she lost her smile. "Did he serve me with more papers? Just send them to legal. I don't even want to look at them today."

Val shook her head. "I don't think legal needs to see it. I opened it. I'm sorry I opened it. I want you to know it's not your fault. It's on your desk. I didn't want anyone else to see it. They might get the wrong idea."

The wrong idea? About what? Her heart clenched and she strode through the doors to her office. What the hell had he done now?

"Amy? Do I need to take a look at it? If it's got something to do with the lawsuit, I might need to see it." Liam followed her in.

She frowned down because it was a bunch of black and white pictures of her and Flynn. It looked like someone had been following them around. There was a picture of her holding his hand as he led her out of a restaurant. There was one of her smiling as she got into his car. There were several of them walking into Flynn's building.

"Why would he think anyone would care about pictures of me with my boyfriend?" She flipped through them. It looked like he'd also left a note at the bottom of the pile.

"Because I got a bad feeling your boyfriend's been lying to you." Liam stared down at the pictures. "I didn't think anything about it. I don't know a lot about Flynn, but I'm putting it together now. How much access has he had to your computer?"

She held the letter in her hand, but she looked up at Liam. "What? Why would you ask that?"

Liam pulled out his phone. "Erin, I need you to get me a report on John Flynn Adler. I think there's likely a junior in there. Yes, I'm talking about Mitch's brother. He's been running some kind of a scam on Amy Slaten. I need everything you can find on the bastard. No. It's not a conflict of interest. Amy's our client. If Mitch has a problem with it, we can discuss it later. As a matter of fact, I'll likely have that discussion with him whether he likes it or not. Get back to me as soon as you can. Slaten might have a leak we need to plug and fast."

It seemed as if the temperature in the room dropped by ten degrees. John Flynn Adler? "His name is John Flynn. He's not…there's no way."

Liam had to be wrong. Flynn was a coder. He wrote software. He didn't run a company. He sure as hell didn't run Glendale. That guy was out in California. He definitely wasn't Flynn. Though her Flynn had admitted to moving out here recently.

He wouldn't do that to her. He cared about her.

He'd shown up at her place the night before a big meeting. He'd never been to her place except to pick her up or drop her off, but yesterday he'd insisted on spending the night. He'd put her to bed and he could have done anything he'd wanted to. She wasn't good with computers, but he was a master. He could easily have gotten into her

147

system and found out what she was doing. He would likely have thought he had more time because no one signed a deal within hours of a proposal. He would have sent all the information back to his company and they would try to counter her.

But he wouldn't do that because he wasn't John Adler. He couldn't be.

"I'm going to take care of this," Liam assured her. "I need to take your laptop and get it to Adam. We need to see if he's been in your system. Did you ever bring him here to the office?"

She shook her head, completely numb. All day long she'd had a delicious ache in her backside. She hadn't minded because it reminded her of Flynn and how he'd taken her and given to her.

Had it all been an act? She'd told him last night all about the company and all about what she was going through. How could he not know who she was?

That was it. He didn't know. She hadn't known. And she'd started out using her married name. That was it. She breathed a deep sigh of relief. He was confused.

But she'd told him the night before. She'd told him she was Amy Slaten and her company was Slaten Industries and he hadn't blinked an eye.

He hadn't stopped and shaken his head and asked her to say it again. He hadn't said anything. They'd talked about Glendale and John Adler, Jr. He hadn't explained that they were talking about him.

"Are you all right?" Liam asked.

No. She wasn't all right. She was numb. Totally numb. That was good. It was far better than screaming and crying. She wasn't going to do that. "I'm fine. A little surprised."

"This could all be a mistake, you know."

But it wasn't. It couldn't be. Not after she'd told him outright. It was funny really. She'd always hated her last name until he'd called her Ms. Lyndon and she'd realized she wanted to hear it from Flynn's lips. When he'd called her Ms. Slaten, it hadn't been so bad.

She glanced down at the note her father had left her.

How will the board feel when they find out you've been sleeping with the enemy? When I'm done filling them all in, they'll call for a vote. Especially after they hear the rumor that you're about to be investigated by the FTC. Sometimes, dear daughter, the enemy of my enemy is my friend. See you in a few weeks.

Liam's phone trilled but she didn't truly hear it or the conversation that took place. All she could hear was the way Flynn said her name and how crazy he was about her.

All lies.

"Amy? You went pale," Liam said. "Erin's on her way over with Adam. We're going to fix this. I promise. There's nothing he could have done that we can't fix."

Oh, but there was no fixing what he'd done to her.

She nodded. "Of course."

She sat down and went back to work. Years of pretending had taught her how to look perfectly placid on the outside while she was dying on the inside.

Plans. Her father had them. Flynn had them. It was time to make a few of her own.

* * * *

"So we can get it done?" Flynn asked, looking over at his brother.

The afternoon sun flooded in, illuminating the stacks of papers, reports, and binders filled with corporate law that Mitch had been using all day to try to get Flynn out of the mess he found himself in.

After he'd dropped Amy off, he'd called his brother and they'd been holed up in Flynn's condo ever since.

He had to find a way to make this right. He had to or he would lose her and suddenly losing her seemed like the end of the fucking world. Not getting to hold her, to cuddle with her and comfort her seemed like a black hole of an existence.

God, he hadn't realized how much he loved her until he'd realized he could lose her.

Mitch rubbed a spot on his forehead as though trying to stave off a headache. "We can do it but it's going to cost you and you'll very likely have to go back to California during the transition."

He hadn't thought about that. If he ousted Hamilton, he would have to run the company until he could find another CEO.

Mitch had gone over all the pros and cons of getting rid of their rogue CEO. Naturally he'd done it in the most sarcastic way possible. He'd made a list.

Cons—probable stock devaluation, employee and customer unrest, possible lawsuit

Pros—Flynn's dick might not get left in the cold

Yeah, his brother was a giver.

"I can find another CEO very quickly." He still had the candidates from the last search on speed dial. One of them would do.

Mitch turned serious eyes on him. "You're playing fast and loose with a lot of people's jobs, Flynn. I know this sounds insane since you're doing this all for her, but Amy Slaten would never do this."

"I wouldn't want her to." He didn't like how Mitch's words were making him feel. He hadn't wanted any of this responsibility. He'd never liked management, wasn't suited for it at all. "Amy's better than I am. She's good at her job. She gives a damn, which is precisely why I can't allow my CEO to try to ruin her."

Mitch groaned. "He's not trying to ruin her. He's playing hardball. She'll counter punch and the game will go on. It's the way business works. Hamilton isn't doing anything a thousand CEOs haven't done before."

"She wouldn't do it." He knew it deep down. Amy wouldn't play fast and loose with her morality. She would be forthright and she would play fair.

"I agree with you, but I can also assure you that lighting a torch to Glendale won't fix the situation. Sit her down. Explain what happened. Hell, tell her what Hamilton did and help her come up with a way to maneuver out of the trap. There's a reason he wants her out. She's a much better executive than her father ever thought of being. Hamilton's scared of her."

He should be. She was smart and determined. All she really needed was the right support. A man who would stand beside her and make sure she knew she was loved.

That was the job he wanted. He wanted to be the man behind the woman. He could do the work he was passionate about and ensure Amy had a happy home to return to each night because she would bear the burden of running the business.

One big business.

His employees deserved the very best CEO he could give them. They deserved her.

"What are the ramifications of merging Glendale with Slaten?" Flynn heard himself asking.

Mitch's head fell back and he groaned, though it wasn't an unhappy sound. "He learns. Thank god. The ramifications are you become way less of an asshole, the company gets an amazing leader, and I don't have to worry that Will is going to murder me. So yes, that is what we should start talking about doing."

Flynn breathed a deep sigh of relief. The answer had been staring him in the face the whole time. Amy was a brilliant executive who cared deeply about her company and employees.

Could she care about his, too? Could she make it hers?

"I'm going to run some numbers and see where the redundancies would fall." It was the first time Mitch had smiled all day. "You were actually planning an expansion so I'm hoping we wouldn't lose any jobs in a merger, simply shift employees around and let older employees choose very nice early retirement packages if they like."

"She has to say yes."

"Convince her," Mitch shot back. "She doesn't have to marry you. This is about what's best for both companies. Naturally you'll also have to have a very close working relationship with her, and if that leads to more intimacy and eventually marriage, then good all around."

"You're a manipulative bastard, Mitch. And way more romantic than I gave you credit for." It could work. He would sit her down, explain the situation and give her the solution. She might be a little angry at first, but she had a good head on her shoulders. It would be all right.

There was a chime that let him know someone with a code was coming up. Only a few people had the code to his private elevator and he wasn't set to pick up Amy for a few hours.

"Is Chase out of class early today?" Flynn asked.

Mitch shrugged. "No idea. You should probably tell him you're going to merge Glendale with your sub's company. He'll be thrilled. He doesn't want the job any more than you do."

At least he didn't have to worry about his brothers being upset about handing over a multimillion-dollar company to his girlfriend.

But one day that girl was going to be his wife. He just knew it.

The doors opened and he felt a smile cross his face. Amy walked out of the elevator, still dressed for her meeting.

And then his smile died because the expression on her face was a careful blank and she wasn't alone. Liam O'Donnell stood beside her and he wasn't bothering with a blank expression. He looked thunderously angry.

Mitch cursed and stood up. "Li, I can explain."

"You fucking better be able to, Mitch, because you know how Big Tag is going to handle this. You better be damn happy I'm the one on your doorstep and not him. Fuck all. You know he can't handle this shite right now and here ya are, helping your brother scam my bloody client." The Irishman continued his curse-filled rant.

Flynn felt the bottom drop out of his world. He wasn't sure how she'd found out, but she definitely knew he'd kept something from her. He turned to Amy. "Baby, we need to talk."

She looked through him. "I only came along with Li because I left a few things here. I'll get them and then I'll be out of your way. You and your brother can continue with whatever meeting you were having."

She started to walk back toward the bedroom, ignoring him utterly. He hated the blank expression on her face, loathed how shut down she was. This was supposed to be her big day. Win or lose she was supposed to feel something, and it looked like she was completely ice cold.

He'd done that to her.

"What happened? How did you find out?"

Her voice was as cold as her expression. "How did I find out you were playing me? Well, I learned it the way I learn all the hard lessons in my life. I learned it from my father. I suppose you weren't afraid of him outing you because you already knew what he was doing."

The words stopped him in his tracks. "What do you mean?"

She kept going. "He's been following me. I guess you made it easy for his PIs. Having an affair with you won't go over well with my board. I'll either be conspiring against my own company or too stupid to realize I was sleeping with the enemy."

He had to jog to catch up with her. What had her father done? If he found out Hamilton had anything to do with this, he would kill the fucker himself. "We're not enemies. Our fathers might have been, but we're not. You and me. We're Flynn and Amy and not our dads."

She opened a drawer and pulled out a pair of pajamas she'd left there. He'd liked her having a drawer. He wanted her to take up half the space. He wanted to open his closet and see her clothes hanging alongside his. "No, you're worse than your father. From what I can tell your dad merely reacted to mine being a complete dick. I'm sure he did something awful to start the feud."

"He slept with my father's first wife."

She turned, her eyes flaring. "So you decided to pay my dad back by fucking his daughter? I could have told you that wouldn't work. He doesn't care about me. The minute I broke with him I became less than an insect to that man. All he wants to do now is step on me and be done with it."

At least there was some emotion in her now. "I would never do that. Not to any woman much less one I care about."

"It's over Flynn. I got Clannahan to sign so if you're trying to protect your place with me so you can torch my negotiations, you're too late."

He smiled, a real genuine relief. "You got them? Baby, I can't tell you how happy I am about that."

Dark eyes rolled as she reached for the bracelet she'd left on the dresser top. "Sure you are. What's the game now? You didn't get Clannahan so you're trying to find another angle."

He'd found his angle. "There's no game here. There's just one insanely stupid man. I should have told you in the beginning. I recognized you. I knew who you were. I went to Sanctum on that first night to explain to Wade why I couldn't be your training Dom."

"You didn't explain very well, did you?" Sarcasm dripped from her mouth.

He ignored it. She deserved a few digs. "I saw you and I knew I had to have you. No matter what the cost was. At the time I thought the cost would all be mine because I was absolutely certain you were the one playing me."

She snorted. "Now you know. I'm far too stupid to ever win a game with you, Adler."

"No games, Amy. I wasn't lying. I saw you and I knew I had to try with you. God, do you think I get that jealous of all the women I've recently met? I acted like an idiot that day because something deep inside me had already connected with you. You kissed me and it was more erotic and intimate than all the women I'd slept with before you."

"Don't bother. It's not going to work."

But her face had flushed and her breathing had picked up. He moved in, taking up more space. She held her ground as he got closer.

"It has to work. It has to because you're so fucking important to me."

Her eyes were on his chest, as though she didn't dare trade stares with him. "If I was, then you would have told me. You thought I was trying to steal your software, didn't you?"

"At first. Your father sent a lot of spies our way, pet."

"Don't call me that," she demanded, her voice rough with emotion. Finally, some emotion.

"All right, I'll stop for now, but know I'm using it in my head because I can't think of you and not want to pet you, not want to have you curled in my lap and purring in my arms."

Now those eyes came up, flashing fire. "Yes, I suppose I did seem like an idiot kitten to you, didn't I?"

"Not at all." He had to stay calm. He wanted to force her to listen to him, but he had to use persuasion. It was everything he'd been afraid of. Maybe in order to get past his lie it was time for him to start telling her the truth. No matter how vulnerable it made him. "You're everything, Amy. I did worry you'd manipulated your way into my house so you could take the software. It's everything I've been working on for years and I still risked it because I wanted you so badly."

"Or you wanted to catch me."

He shook his head. "I wanted you."

"So you didn't watch me carefully? I should have known there was a reason you insisted on taking me to and from work and spending all your free time with me."

"That was because I was already crazy about you. I didn't want to spend a minute away from you."

She wasn't having it. "Did you or did you not put security measures in place after that first morning?"

He winced, but he was determined to be nothing but honest with her from now on. He'd fucked it up so badly. "I had Simon Weston put in some cameras because it looked like someone had tried to get into the tower to take the drive. It turned out to be not a screwdriver but my housekeeper's old vacuum cleaner. It had some metal parts and she scratched it up when she was trying to clean the rug around it. I felt so stupid I bought her a new one."

"You took video?"

"Yeah, but only until I figured out what had happened." He realized what she was worried about and shook his head immediately. They'd made love at his desk. "No, baby. There was a tiny camera and it was at the same level as the tower. No one could see more than legs. I swear."

She'd turned a brilliant shade of pink. "You're a bastard. Whoever watched those tapes knew. They knew what we were doing."

"I watched them. I definitely knew what we were doing because I was there. Simon loaned me the cameras as a favor. I did all the surveillance."

"And who ran all the checks on me?" Amy asked. "According to Adam Miles, someone's run several rather invasive checks into my background and my finances. Were you looking for some kind of payoff for me spying on you?"

At least she was listening. "No and that was all in the beginning. I called off everyone a few weeks ago."

"Everyone except your CEO, who seems to be in league with my father."

"I'm going to fire him. That's what Mitch is doing here today. Go and look at the paperwork. I'm going to pay his ass off and get rid of the fucker because I won't let anyone treat you like that. I didn't realize what he was doing until last night." He moved in again and this time he got his hands on her arms and put his forehead to hers. "We can call him. Hell, I'll let you give him the news. I don't care. I just need you to forgive me. I know I should have told you, but I was happy. God, for the first fucking time in my life I was really happy and I was scared to lose it."

For a second he thought she would turn her face up and let him kiss her, let him put everything he was feeling that second into something physical. He wasn't sure words were enough.

"I can't believe you." She stepped away and moved around him.

He followed her back down the hall. "Think about it, Amy. Why would I lie now except that I truly want you? I've got nothing left to lose. You have the company we were fighting over. I know you won't believe me but I told my CEO to let Clannahan go."

She turned on him. "Is that what you're trying to say? Now it's all your doing that I won the contract?"

That had been a trap he'd fallen into. "Not at all. You won that fair and square and I want to hear all about it. I was praying we could celebrate tonight."

"I'm sure you were. You'll forgive me if I don't see you again. I'm leaving the training program and I expect that you will never contact me."

He reached out for her hand. "Don't do this, Amy."

"Get your hand off her right now," a dark voice said.

"I would do what he says, Flynn. He's got a gun and he won't hesitate to use it." Mitch and Liam O'Donnell were standing in the living room, staring at them. Mitch's face was tight as though he hadn't enjoyed what was likely a very tense conversation with O'Donnell.

He'd gotten his brother in trouble, too.

He dropped Amy's hand, but he couldn't let her go. "Please stay and talk to me."

She turned.

When he tried to follow her, he found a massive Irishman in his way.

"Mr. O'Donnell, this is between me and my sub." He couldn't let her go. Not like this. Maybe not ever.

Mitch cursed under his breath. "You've had your Sanctum membership revoked, Flynn. And Li is here in a professional capacity. He won't back off. He handles security for Slaten. In this case, he's acting as Ms. Slaten's bodyguard."

"She doesn't need a bodyguard." What the hell was happening? How had everything fallen apart in the course of a single afternoon?

"I've been lax," O'Donnell said, his jaw tight. "I'm supposed to protect the company from spies and the head of the company from people who want to use her. I won't make the same mistake again. Ms. Slaten, have you gotten everything you need?"

She nodded, her eyes cold.

"Then why don't you wait for me in the lobby?" O'Donnell asked. "I need to make a few things plain to Mr. Adler."

"Don't walk away," he pleaded.

She turned and was in the elevator. The doors closed and she was gone.

He couldn't breathe. What the fuck had he done?

O'Donnell stared at him. "I need you to understand that if I find you around my employer again, I'll take ya out meself and I won't care a damn that you're Mitch's brother. Do you have any idea the trouble you've caused for him?"

"He didn't know." He had to get Mitch out of this.

"Of course I did," Mitch replied.

"The only reason I'm not pushing to revoke his membership is the fact that he's also your lawyer," O'Donnell continued. "We've got the clusterfuck of a situation that both you and Amy are clients of McKay-Taggart. Simon and Jesse are your liaisons. We'll be having a long meeting to try to figure out if we can reasonably keep both Glendale and Slaten as clients after all this fucking mess."

"Don't you drop her. Please don't drop her. I'll find someone else." He couldn't cost her another thing.

O'Donnell was quiet for a minute and then switched his focus to Mitch. "You weren't kidding, were you?"

Mitch sighed. "I told you this wasn't about business. I'm pretty sure he'd been burned before and he was scared. He's in love with her."

He felt like an idiot standing there between the two older men, but he couldn't lie. "I do love her. I swear I wasn't planning on taking her company. I was going to try to give her mine."

O'Donnell seemed to soften slightly. "So you're nothing but a dumbass. Is that what you're trying to tell me?"

"Mitch is right. I've been stupid. I knew about a week in that she wouldn't spy on me. My fiancée...I found out she was marrying me for money. She took some work product and sold it to a rival company. I'm sure she intended to do much more of that after the wedding. She had a secret account and a secret lover she funneled money to."

"Amy's nothing like that," O'Donnell pointed out.

"I know that, but I…I don't know what I was thinking. After a few weeks, I was just fucking scared to tell her because I knew I'd been wrong. I wanted something to give to her to make up for it somehow. And then she told me how much she hated me. The real me, not the one she knew."

"I doubt that woman could truly hate anyone," Mitch said with a frown. "I don't think she hates you now. I think she's hurt."

"You'll have to forgive Mitchell. He's very good at pointing out the obvious," O'Donnell said with a shake of his head. "You poor bastard. You screwed up with her. I'll let Big Tag know you prefer to leave over her if it comes to that. We don't normally have these kinds of conflicts of interest. You can see why it causes headaches. Look, maybe I was harsh on you but I can't let you around her if she doesn't want you there."

"Her father is coming after her. You have to stop him." He wasn't sure of everything that was going on with her father, but he knew her father wanted his place back and it looked like he was going to use Flynn to further that goal.

He couldn't be the reason she lost her company. Even if he offered her the job at Glendale, it wouldn't make up for losing Slaten. She'd sacrificed for Slaten.

O'Donnell turned to Mitch. "She's got her own lawyers working on that, but I think if the bastard calls a vote, she's going to be short. Unless someone could figure out a way to sway the board. Or perhaps buy up enough stock that they would have a voting share. The way I figure it, she needs two more votes to be safe."

Mitch frowned. "That could cost millions. I mean millions of dollars and with absolutely no guarantee that she would come back to him. She might see it as the beginnings of a hostile takeover. That is if we could even get one of the board members to sell. Slaten used to have a strict no-sell policy to anyone other than family."

O'Donnell continued. "Ah, but Amy thought that was a draconian law. She had it taken out of the bylaws along with the morality codes. And she likely wouldn't see it as a hostile takeover if he signed the stock over to her once he'd voted."

"You can't expect him to do that," Mitch argued. "You're talking about at least ten million. It could be far more than that to get two freaking board votes. He's not going to turn around and hand it over."

"I'll do it." He would have to sell the condo. He would fucking have to sell just about everything, but he knew in an instant none of it mattered if he didn't have her.

God, he had to pray it worked.

The elevator chimed again and he turned to the door as Mitch began to argue against the utterly insane plan. Amy. She was coming back. He could talk to her. He could make her see reason.

Instead, the doors opened and he saw Amy had sicced someone else on him because her brother-in-law entered the room like a bull in search of someone to gore.

Will Daley strode in, still in his scrubs. "You son of a bitch. I swear to god, I'm going to kill you and then I'm going to kill your brother."

Mitch held his hands up. "He's going to pay ten million to buy two board seats so Amy doesn't lose Slaten and then he's going to sign all the stock over to her."

Wow. That had gone down fast. It looked like all Mitch had needed to get on board with Flynn spending his entire fortune on the hopes that a girl would like him was his best friend threatening to kill them all.

Will stopped in the middle of the room. "Are you serious?"

At least he might get one of her family members on his side. "Yes, but you can't tell her because right now she would likely try to block me. She's angry, but I swear I'm going to get her out of this mess and make sure her father can't screw with her ever again. I love her."

"I think you're right about her blocking you," Will said with a frown. "I don't know that she would allow you to save her from drowning right now." He looked to Mitch. "Is it that bad? Could she lose the company?"

Mitch put a hand on his best friend's shoulder. "It's bad, but I think we can accomplish what we need to with one vote."

"I think it's worse than it looks on paper," O'Donnell said with a grimace. "I want him to buy two votes which means he'll need someone else to vote the second share. I was thinking Mitch, but maybe you want to do it. Bridget already has a vote. She's the only one we can count on."

Flynn shook his head. "No. I've got someone else in mind. I'll handle this. I'll make sure she doesn't lose Slaten."

"Are you really going to do this?" Will asked, looking him straight in the eyes.

He had to do it. It would cost him everything he had, but now he realized she was the only thing that mattered. "I'll put the condo on the market tomorrow, but I've heard Simon's cousin wanted to buy it before I did so I'll call Michael Malone tonight and see if I can work out a deal."

He would sell the condo, the cars, anything he had to in order to make sure she was safe.

"I want it in writing that you'll sign the stock over to her at the end. We'll work out some way to pay you, but I can't have you taking over Slaten. If this is some kind of ruse..." Will began.

Flynn shut that shit down. "I don't want to take over Slaten. I want her to take over Glendale. I'll sign whatever you want me to sign. Just keep it quiet until I can give her what she needs."

Will took a deep breath and groaned. "Oh, thank god. Bridget told me I had to come over here and kick some ass or she would, and she's on bed rest. You're lucky she's on bed rest. She wouldn't have stopped to listen to explanations. You're an asshole. That was a shit ton of drama. Someone get me a beer."

Mitch proved he knew where the beer was.

And Flynn prayed it all would work. He was gambling everything but he wouldn't have it any other way.

Of course if they were going to take two board seats, he would need a partner in crime. He could use Mitch, but Amy might see that as a hostile takeover. There was only one man she really trusted. Perhaps if she saw him there, she would trust Flynn, too.

Flynn prepared for what might be the toughest call of his life. Luckily Will had Frankie's number. It was time for the ex-husband and the man who prayed he would be the future husband to have a long talk about the woman they both loved.

Chapter Nine

Amy felt a little sick at the thought of what she had to do.

"It's going to be all right," a voice said over the speaker. Bridget. Her sister sounded calmer than usual. It was odd. Bridget was usually the emotional one. "You have to know that. You're going to walk in and stare him down and let him know he can't beat you."

Their father. He was already in the building. He'd been shown to the boardroom and her security people would ensure he didn't walk around causing trouble. They were the same security people who would very likely be out of a job in less than an hour.

"I think he already has," she said hollowly. She wished her sister was here with her and not just talking through the speakerphone. "Someone's buying up stock. I think Dad bought out our cousins."

A groan came over the line. "Violet and Meryl? Jeez. That's a lot of cash for them to get their claws on. Did they blow it all on cocaine and male hookers?"

She had to laugh despite the gravity of the situation. Bridget had an interesting view of their family life. "I believe Violet needs the cash because the IRS finally figured out she hasn't filed taxes in twelve years, but I'm pretty sure Meryl wants it for her new nineteen-year-old boyfriend. And he probably will buy cocaine with it."

"I knew there was some blow in there somewhere. And the plastic surgeons of Los Angeles probably had a party when they heard the news." She could practically see Bridget fist pump. The line went quiet for a moment. "I really do think you're going to be fine. You're a fighter and you have people who love you very much."

Yes, she had her sister and she had Frankie. "I haven't told him, you know. He has no idea what's going on."

"I think Flynn knows," Bridget replied.

Her whole body tensed. "I wasn't talking about him. I was talking about Frankie."

"Oh. Well, yeah. Uhm, I'm sure he doesn't know."

Her sister was a freaking horrible liar. Even over the phone. "Damn it, Bridget. Tell me you didn't call him."

"I didn't." She sounded confident again, that waver in her voice that always told Amy she was lying gone. "I haven't talked to Frankie since the last time you both came over for dinner. I don't talk to anyone anymore. I lay around and a small soccer player tries to score goals on my bladder. Bed rest sucks. Will won't even let me type right now. I've watched so much HGTV I'm ready to write a ménage about those damn twins."

Her sister was good at deflecting. "What's going on, Bridget?"

There was a pause. "I think you need to give Flynn another chance."

"What? You were the one who told me to cut his balls off with a rusty pair of scissors, toss them out on the lawn, and watch the birds eat them." Her sister had a way with words.

Simply hearing Flynn's name made her heart hurt. She missed him. The last two weeks had gone by in a blur of work and anxiety and way too much crying over that man. She'd done it with her sister. She'd spent more time in Will and Bridget's guest room than she liked to admit. At first it was because she kind of thought Flynn would show up and try to explain himself again. Then it was because he hadn't. He didn't call or text or write her an e-mail. He was gone and that was that.

She thought she would be relieved.

Tears pricked at her eyes, but she wasn't going to shed them. He was done with her. She was done with him. She would concentrate on Slaten…or finding a new job.

If she lost today, she would go back to California and start over. She would forget the man who'd made her feel safe, the one she could be herself with. She would leave it all behind and she would never let another man in again. Never.

"Maybe I was wrong. He's actually quite sweet," Bridget said.

She felt her brow furrow. "When did you see Flynn? You're supposed to be on bed rest."

"He came to see me. Well, I think he mostly came over because Mitch and Will were watching a basketball game and it seems like he's in the process of moving."

Moving? He was leaving that glorious condo of his? Well, maybe it had only been temporary anyway. He was likely moving back to San Francisco where Glendale was located. He'd done his job. He'd gotten everything he could out of her and now he was leaving. It made sense. "And Will let him in?"

She knew that shouldn't hurt so much, but up until earlier in the week, she'd been staying with them to avoid Flynn. Will invited the bastard over? She knew he was friends with Mitch, but couldn't he have waited? She was still going over to see her sister most days. That would have been an awkward situation.

"Will likes him."

She definitely felt the betrayal. Somehow she'd gotten it in her head that maybe, just maybe Flynn was suffering, too. Nope. He was hanging with her brother-in-law and enjoying some guy time. Asshole. "Awesome. I hope they'll be very happy together. I'll make sure I call from now on to see if he's visiting. I wouldn't want things to be weird."

A long sigh came over the line. "Amy, this isn't like you."

"What? Not enjoying my own humiliation? I can see where you would say that since I've had so much of it in my life."

"No, this negativity. It's not like you. Even when Dad was doing his worst, you stayed upbeat. You were always the positive one."

She had to be because Bridget could be relentlessly negative at times. One of them had to see the positive side of life. Her sister had found her true joy when she'd married Will and that darkness was gone, so now Amy could let some pessimism in. "No, I showed you what I wanted to show you. I didn't let you see me cry back then."

"But you let him," Bridget said quietly.

"How do you know that?" Those sessions had been private.

"Because he told me. Because he knows a you that I don't know and that's because you loved him enough to let those walls down. Amy, I know it's hard. I really do. I never thought I would get married and have a kid because our childhood fucked me over, too. But Will managed to get through and I think Flynn got through to you."

He'd gotten through to her. He'd ripped her heart right out of her chest and kicked it to the curb. "It's a totally different thing, Bridget. Will was afraid of long-term commitment. He didn't lie to you about his name and motives. Flynn played me."

"Not according to him." Bridget's voice had gone soft.

"He lies."

"He did in the beginning but you have to know Dad fucked with his head, too," Bridget pointed out. "I talked at length with him about the Glendale side of this feud. Dad was a bastard who took every opportunity to screw Flynn's dad over. Everyone thought you would continue on with the family hobby. Did you know Dad sent one of his old employees out to Glendale to tell their CEO exactly that? He sent the old head of security out to fuck around with Glendale and make you look bad."

"Ray Paulsen? That doesn't surprise me." She could even see the plotting behind it now. If Glendale thought she was going to continue the feud, they would come at her hard when she was in her first year. That would be her most vulnerable time. The chaos all the conflict with Glendale could produce would shake faith in her and give her father a better chance at getting back his job.

It was a dick move, but then her father wrote the dick move playbook.

"Flynn says he's been telling the Glendale CEO all sorts of tales about how you're working against them and spying. The CEO brought his paranoia to Flynn. He honestly thought you knew who he was and you were using him."

She could give him that in the beginning. Unfortunately, she'd proven him so very wrong and he still hadn't come forward. "And when he figured out I was nothing more than an idiot?"

"Men are stupid. They get comfortable and they don't think about the future. They're only capable of thinking about two minutes ahead. He thought he had time to fix things. He knew he'd screwed up royally and he got scared."

Why on earth had Flynn had this discussion with her sister? What angle was he playing now? Why wouldn't he try to talk to her?

"There's nothing to fix. I can't trust him. And you know he hasn't exactly tried to apologize to me. He might be hanging with Will, but I haven't heard from him at all."

"I think he's kind of a big gesture guy," Bridget said. "He was waiting until he could make his big gesture."

"No gesture is going to work on me." She could hear the stubbornness in her voice, but she had to question it since she'd spent days praying he would call and come up with something that would make his betrayal forgivable.

What would work? Could she ever believe him again? Work would always come between them.

Except she was about to get the boot and then she wouldn't work for the enemy anymore.

"If this big gesture doesn't work for you, then you probably will be alone for the rest of your life, sister. Because this one is epic and you have no idea how hard it's been not to tell you about it. I wish I could be there in person. It isn't often a Dom hands over his balls in quite so public a fashion. Take care of them. Balls are actually quite delicate."

"What are you talking about?"

"You'll see. I'm hanging up now so I can call into the conference room. Will's in emergency surgery so I'm calling in our vote. I wonder who I'll vote for? Evil Dad or my beautiful princess sister. It's a mystery. Stay tuned."

The line went dead.

She stared at the phone wondering what the hell her sister had meant by that.

"The meeting is supposed to start in two minutes," Val said, poking her head in the room. "Do you need me to delay?"

Her stomach did a slow somersault. Was there any reason to delay the inevitable? "Is everyone here? Or at least their proxies?"

Since she'd moved the company to Texas, her aunt only sent proxies out to vote for her. Aunt Beverly thought Dallas was still the Wild West and refused to even touch down at the airport. She believed that New York, Los Angeles, and Paris were the only cities in the world worth being in. The good news was the proxy didn't typically insult Amy's wardrobe choices and make snide comments about her gaining weight.

God, she hated her family sometimes.

Why had she thought she could start a new one?

"The last two board members are on their way up. I've been told they've cleared security and should be here any second."

They would do her father's will. He'd likely nominally put the shares under their names so he could control the vote. They would be paid off and the shares would be used as a cattle prod to keep everyone in line. Her father now owned enough board seats to never have to worry about Amy or anyone else kicking him out again.

He would eventually use those shares and those votes to sell the company, and all the work she'd done with Clannahan would be for nothing.

She wondered if Glendale would sweep in and scoop them up. Would Flynn be celebrating? She grabbed her bag. Her father would very likely have her walked out of the building. "Let's go and get this done."

Val nodded, her face a tight mask. "Yes, let's finish this off. I'll be waiting for you if you need anything."

Val was being kind. Amy started down the hallway that would take her past the lobby and into the conference room where she would find her fate. Waterloo. It was her Waterloo and it looked like she was playing Napoleon this time. "I would like for you to pack up my office if the need arises."

"Yes, ma'am."

"And my father will bring in his own assistant. I'm so sorry about that, but I've ensured you get six months pay. Take it before he realizes what I've done and countermands the order," Amy instructed. "HR will be waiting for you. They'll cut a check then and there."

Sometimes she had to move fast to get her will done. She wished she'd realized that before this moment.

"Do you really think this is going to happen?" Val hurried to keep up with her.

"Yes. We need to prepare ourselves." She needed to be ready, to stand tall.

God, she wanted to see him. The need washed over her like a tidal wave. Flynn. He was a rat-fink bastard and all she wanted was for him to be right here, right now. She wouldn't talk to him, wouldn't promise him anything, but she would ask him to pretend for a moment. She would ask him to pretend it had been real, that he'd loved her the way she'd loved him.

She could fool herself all she liked. She loved him. He was there in her heart, a weed she couldn't bring herself to pull. It was a damn good thing he hadn't shown up on her doorstep because she likely would have bought his bullshit.

She missed Flynn and her friends at the club. They would all be graduating and moving on with their lives. They would get together on weekends and play and explore and she…wouldn't. She would move back to California and find new work. She would throw herself into it and forget about all her other needs. If she ever took another lover, she would be in control. Submission would be something she merely dreamed about because she would never take another Dom. He'd been it for her.

Amy stopped outside the door.

"Are you all right?" Val asked.

She couldn't. God, she couldn't walk through that door yet. She pulled out her cell and dialed the number she'd promised she wouldn't dial ever again.

What was she going to say? *Please, Flynn. Just tell me it's going to be all right. Tell me I'm going to be all right. I can do it if I hear your voice.*

She heard his unique ringtone and stopped. He'd changed her ringtone on his phone so when she called him he could tell it was her. It was a chiming sound because he told her talking to her soothed him.

"Amy?"

She hung up because she'd heard his voice and not through the damn phone. He'd sounded like he was on the other side of the door.

Oh god, how wrong had she been about him? How bad was it? He was here and what the hell did that mean?

She pushed the door open and there he was, sitting at the conference table, looking like sin in a suit. His hair was slicked back, his face clean-shaven. He'd dressed for the occasion.

Someone had bought her cousin's seats on the board. She wondered why her father hadn't shoved it in her face.

Glendale was about to take over Slaten.

Or was he here for something else?

167

"Does she look totally surprised?" Bridget's voice came over a speaker. The conference room phone was sitting beside Flynn.

"I think she's definitely surprised," Flynn replied, not moving his stare from her.

"Would you describe it as happy surprise or angry surprise," Bridget continued. "I need description. Use your words."

Amy ignored her sister for the moment because she was mostly shocked surprised. What would a grand gesture look like to Flynn? How would he say he was sorry?

"I want to know what the hell that fucker is doing here."

In the shock of finding Flynn in her conference room, she'd managed to miss her father. He was standing at the back of the room, staring her way. He was dressed up, too, looking every bit the business-man in his prime. But his face was flushed a nice shade of red.

Her father wasn't a good actor and Flynn wouldn't work with him. He might have lied to her, but she was sure he wasn't working with her dad. Certainly she'd accused him of it, but then the day she'd learned who he was, she'd pretty much accused him of anything she possibly could. For the first week, she'd called him every name in the book and would have believed he was the second coming of Satan himself.

Then she'd thought about everything he'd done for her. He hadn't needed to. She'd been perfectly ready to fall into his bed. Not once had he asked to go to her place. He'd preferred having her in his world. Shouldn't he have tried to get into her office? Borrowed her computer?

He hadn't done any of those things.

Was he really that stupid? Could he have found himself in a trap and not realized how to get out?

Or had this been his endgame and the sex had just been a way of lording it over her?

Do you have any idea how good you make me feel?

Had that been all about sex? Or had he been talking about something more?

"I'm asking you a question," her father said, moving toward her.

"You're being an asshole," Bridget shouted over the line.

"You stay out of this." Her dad looked like he wanted to hang up that phone, but he thought better of it since Flynn was guarding it. "I have no idea why your sister allowed you any stock at all, much less a voting share. One more ridiculous move she made. I thought you were smarter than this, Amy. I will not allow you to bring my company down."

Flynn stood immediately, but someone else put his big body between her and her father.

"Don't you even think about touching her." Frankie. She would know those broad shoulders anywhere.

She'd been so intent on staring at Flynn that she hadn't noticed Frankie sitting there.

"Get out of my way," her father said. "You don't belong here either. Unless she talked you into marrying her again. Business is the only way that little bitch can find a husband. I guess you don't care that she's been fucking around with that one over there. She's not exactly your type, is she?"

Flynn started toward him, but Frankie held a hand out. "Don't. We'll never get this done if you're in jail, Flynn. He's all talk. Ignore him. Treat him like a troll on the Internet. Don't feed him."

"Punch him instead." Bridget had always been a little bloodthirsty.

"You can't hit him." Her father would sue Flynn in a heartbeat and they wouldn't get through this meeting.

"I'll let it go for now, but I swear if he says one nasty thing about my...about Amy, I'll spend the rest of my life making his hell," Flynn promised.

"See, Amy, he's totally likable." Bridget chuckled over the line.

"He might be." Amy couldn't take her eyes off him. He was here. Right here. It was as though she'd conjured the man in her darkest hour.

"If you think for a second that you can take my company, you bastard, you're wrong." Her father seemed to find a better target in Flynn.

"It's not your company," Flynn shot back.

"It will be once the rest of the board gets here." Her father strode back and forth, looking out the glass windows as if waiting for someone.

He was waiting on Violet and Meryl. He didn't know they'd sold their stock. He didn't know he'd lost their votes.

"He looks angry surprised, right? Damn it. I miss all the good stuff," Bridget huffed.

Amy glanced back at Flynn. He looked so good it almost hurt to stare at him.

"What are you doing here?" She kept her voice down, well aware that she was surrounded by members of her family and they lived to gossip.

"Trying to make amends. Start the meeting. I want to get this over with. I know you're nervous, but I'm nervous, too. I want to find out what happens next. I need to know. It's been killing me." He turned and walked back to his seat. He was sitting between her uncle and a man who had to be her aunt's proxy. Frankie took the seat beside where the CEO sat.

What happened next? She wasn't so sure what was happening right now. And why was her ex-husband here?

"Why are you here, Frankie?"

"I should have been called the minute it all went wrong," Frankie said with a frown. "The only reason I even know you're in trouble is Flynn. You didn't let me help you so I helped him. Now go and start this meeting. Flynn's right. We need to get this over with as soon as possible."

Frankie was helping him? Frankie winked her way. What exactly had they done? What were they going to do?

A calm came over her as she looked at Flynn.

What kind of man was he, really? She'd spent weeks with him, gotten to know him intimately. Who was this man? He'd lied to her. He'd tricked her. He'd thought she was the enemy at one point. He'd given her what she needed. He'd held her while she cried.

He'd made it possible for her to cry.

Why would he be here today? Why would he have bought the board seat? Seats? Frankie's money was like hers—tied up in the company at this point. Her mind worked, calculating how much two voting seats could possibly have cost. At the very least fifteen million. If her cousins negotiated at all, likely twenty.

Flynn had twenty million just lying around?

His condo. Bridget said he was in the process of moving. Had he sold his condo in order to buy the Slaten stock she needed to retain her job?

She moved to the head of the table, her heart starting to pound. Whatever happened now changed everything. Flynn glanced up at her, his eyes locking with hers.

What kind of man was he?

He was the kind of man who would try to make up for his mistake with a massive gesture. He was the kind of man who might be dumb enough to want a woman so much he lived in a dream world where he let go of reality and prayed for the best. Flynn was a dreamer. She was the realist. He needed her to watch over him while he did all the crazy imaginative things his brilliant brain could do.

He was her knight in a pocket protector.

He was here to save her. She knew it suddenly. It was right there in his eyes.

She was fucking going to win.

She stood in front of her board. "I call to order this meeting of the Slaten Industries board of directors, the purpose to vote on the confidence or non-confidence of the CEO. I must recuse myself for the simple fact that I am CEO. Can we vote to forego everything but the vote? I need an aye or nay."

She easily got the go-ahead for the vote, though her father dissented. No one it seemed wanted to go through all the ritual procedure associated with meetings of this kind.

Amy ignored him. "Then we'll get on with it."

Her father stood back up. "No. I want to understand where your cousins are and why those two are here now."

Flynn sent him a grim grin. "I bought them out so you should stop waiting for them to show up. Because of the way your daughter rewrote the company bylaws, I've signed over a voting portion of the stock I own to Frankie. Your daughter is very egalitarian and doesn't want any one person to have too much power so I had to work around her."

Her father nearly went purple. "You can't do this."

"Call the vote." There was a definite bounce to her sister's tone, as though she was perfectly satisfied with what was about to happen.

She didn't hesitate. This vote was going to go her way. "This is a vote of confidence for Amy Slaten as chief executive officer of Slaten Industries. I need an aye or a nay."

"Aye." Bridget gave her the only vote she'd thought she would have.

"Nay," her father said, looking at her uncle. "I say nay."

Her Uncle Jasper wouldn't meet her eyes. "Nay."

She'd expected that.

Her aunt's proxy looked like a young male model. "I'm supposed to read a statement before giving Beverly Slaten's vote." He looked down at his tablet. "I don't like Amy. She's a little prick who thinks she's smarter than everyone else and who doesn't dress for her body type." The proxy grimaced. "Sorry, I'm supposed to read this in order to get paid. I think you're lovely."

So her aunt still managed to get the dig in. "Proceed so we can get this over with."

She didn't need her aunt's vote.

The pretty boy nodded and went back to his tablet. "Still, it turns out she's very likely right and she is smarter than the majority of nitwits who make up this family. Her sister writes porn and her cousins think Tweeting is some form of social justice. She's certainly smarter than her father, who can't keep it in his pants and would sell the company and its revenue out from under us. Did you think I wouldn't find out? Screw you, George. My vote is aye."

"It's called erotic romance, Aunt Beverly," Bridget said. "Not that you would know what an orgasm is. I swear the woman made her money by shoving lumps of coal up her tight ass and shitting out diamonds."

The proxy grinned. "She also says a bunch of stuff about how everyone is disinvited to Thanksgiving and Christmas, and then there's a bunch of paragraphs about how she would like you to die, Mr. Slaten, but it's surprisingly graphic. Can we just say I read it?"

Amy gave him a thumbs-up. She moved to Frankie.

"Aye," he said with the sweetest smile.

They'd started this together and he was still with her. Her sweet friend. She'd worried the way she'd felt about Frankie all the years had ruined her for men, but now she realized her heart was so much bigger than she'd thought it was. It was a massive thing and it could heal quite quickly for the right man.

"And you, Mr. Adler. What say you?" She looked at him, feeling the connection over the distance that separated them.

"Aye," he said, his eyes soft on her. "I will always have confidence in Amy Slaten. So much that I want to offer her my company as well. It seems I'm down a CEO. I can't think of a single person better suited to watch over a merger and ensure both firm's employees are treated with kindness and fairness."

Oh, when that man made a grand gesture, he did it on a massive scale. She had to take a breath at the thought of what he was asking her to do.

Her father stood again, fists clenched at his sides. "You'll never convince the board to merge."

Flynn didn't take his eyes off her. "I will when I explain that my software is almost done and by merging our companies we'll be able to take it to market across the globe and we'll make a billion dollars together. You and me. I'm going to need it because I find myself seriously cash poor."

Frankie nodded, winking her way. "He's sleeping on his brother's couch."

"See, grand gesture on an epic scale." Bridget sighed as though it was all too lovely.

So he had sold the condo. "You are insane."

"And I'll sue." Her father didn't seem to get that this was a very romantic moment. But then again, he was the king of the dick move. "I'll sue both of you."

Flynn just smiled her way, his eyes steady as if he couldn't stop looking at her. "Luckily I know a good lawyer."

"He's going to use you to take us over and obliterate this company." Her father changed tactics and came after her. "Can't you see that?"

Maybe it was far past time to ask him some simple questions. "You going to ruin me, Flynn?"

"No, baby. I need you far too much to ever do that. I'm going to sign over every bit of stock I own in Slaten to you and then I'm going to push for a merger. I have a presentation and everything," he said quietly.

"He's got a very nice PowerPoint ready for you," Frankie agreed. "I approved it myself. I happen to know you prefer graphics and charts in your presentations. He wanted to make sure he also used your favorite colors."

She could almost see Flynn asking Frankie that. A smile started to creep over her face. "Did you really sell the condo?"

"I did. I sold everything except my computers and my stock in Glendale. I need that. You should understand that once I sign the Slaten stock back to you, I'm not worth as much as I used to be. You're going to be the big net worth in this relationship. Everything I have is tied up in Glendale. I have to make sure the company makes it. I need to put it and my future in the hands of the only woman in the world I trust."

"You're going to make this hard on a girl, aren't you?" How the hell could she stay mad at a man who'd put everything on the line for her?

"I have to make it impossible because nothing is more important to me than getting you back and getting the one job in the world I want more than anything."

She was going to cry. She was going to do it in front of everyone and make a fool of herself. "Don't say it."

He got out of his seat and moved toward her. "I have to. I didn't say what I should have said before. I should have taken one look at you and put my hand in yours and given you everything I had. I didn't. I was foolish and awkward and arrogant. I love you, Amy Slaten. The only job in the world I want is to be your husband."

"See," Bridget said, sniffling audibly. "I told you he was sweet."

So freaking sweet. "The ayes have it. I remain the CEO of Slaten Industries. Please let us have the room. And get the security guards if that one won't leave."

Frankie was already moving her father out. "He'll leave or I'll drag him out myself. Move it."

The room emptied and she was finally alone with him.

"What did you do?" It was completely insane. No one would do what he'd done. No one in their right mind gave up everything to maybe get another shot with a woman they'd slept with.

But maybe, just maybe a really crazy man would do it for another shot at a woman he loved.

Flynn moved in but didn't touch her. "I've been miserable without you. I can't sleep. I don't want to eat or work. I need you in my life. Any way you'll have me."

Crazy man. "You think if I take over the CEO job for Glendale Slaten, I'll fall in love with you because we'll be in close proximity."

"Glendale Slaten? I like the sound of that," he admitted. "And I hope you'll fall in love with me because I'm so madly in love with you."

"There's only one problem with that scenario, Adler."

He winced at the way she said his name. "If it helps, I really am called Flynn by absolutely everyone who knows me. And if there's a problem, I'll handle it. I'll do what it takes."

Did he honestly believe she would put him through more hoops? Her whole being felt suffused with joy. He was truly here with her this time. No playing around. There was no way that man was lying to her this time. "I don't think you can solve this problem, Mr. Adler."

That didn't mean she wouldn't drag this out a little.

His jaw went tight and he finally reached for her. "I can't let you go. I'll work every single day to make it up to you. I swear, Amy, I'm going to spend the rest of my life trying to get you back."

She moved into his arms because she couldn't hold out on this man. Her whole body responded to his nearness. "You can't make me fall in love with you because I'm already there, Flynn."

He hauled her into his arms, his lips finding hers. He kissed her over and over again, drugging her with his love.

"I couldn't lose you, pet. I love you too much. Stay with me," he whispered against her lips.

"I love you." It felt so good to finally say it.

"Could y'all talk a little louder?"

Flynn groaned and moved over to the phone. "I think we need some privacy."

They definitely needed some. They had two companies to merge and she knew exactly how she wanted to celebrate. With a merger of her own. "Good-bye, Bridget."

"Damn it. It was just getting good." The line went dead.

Amy walked to the glass windows and started to pull down the shades. Her sister had no idea how good it was going to get. "I think we should take a private meeting, Mr. Adler. If we're going to work together, you should know what I expect."

His hand went to his tie. "Oh, I think we should definitely talk about expectations, Ms. Slaten. I think you'll find they're quite high. If you're going to be my CEO, we should set some rules, perhaps agree to a mutually beneficial contract."

He was so gorgeous and he was all hers. "I think we can come to an agreement. Though it might take a while."

When the door was locked, she went about negotiating in the sexiest way possible.

Epilogue

Flynn opened the door to the hospital room with a smile on his face. It grew wider when he saw his gorgeous fiancée pacing the floor with a bundle in her arms.

She looked good with a baby cuddled close.

One day it would be theirs. Today it was his almost nephew.

"Flynn, welcome back." Will looked up from his place on the small sofa near the hospital bed.

He'd come straight from the airport. He'd been in San Francisco at Glendale getting everything ready for the new CEO's meeting with the staff next week. They were going to love her. "I came straight here. I knew Amy would be here with that little guy."

"Little?" Bridget shook her head, but she was smiling as she looked at her son. "He weighed nine pounds. The only kid in the hospital who was bigger is Erin's boy and he's a Taggart. They're all giants. Will is perfectly normal sized. Why did he have to make a linebacker baby?"

Flynn stepped close to his girl, kissing her cheek before staring down at the baby, who looked awfully small to him. "I think he's beautiful."

Amy practically glowed as she looked up at him. "He is. Brendon Glen Daley. He's such a sweetie."

Flynn couldn't help but move behind her, putting his arms around her. He was in the same room with her. He needed her touch. Always. "I think I'll be a fabulous stay-at-home dad one day."

"Really?" She grinned up at him. "You think you can code with a baby in your arms."

It was a problem he could work on. "I'll type with one hand."

"I'll pay for that show." She kissed her nephew's head and passed him back to her sister.

Bridget cuddled her son close. "How did the merger meeting go?"

"We're a go." After he'd made his presentation and gone over Amy's goals for the company, the board had voted unanimously to move forward with the plan.

Everything was falling into place.

"And the FTC investigation?" Will asked.

He shook his head. "It was all bogus. I've cleaned house and no one is coming after her again. My former CEO was too much like my father when it came to business. I loved my dad, but I think he enjoyed the game too much. I want some peace in my life."

"And George?" Will asked.

"My father is an idiot," Bridget interjected. "We don't have to worry about him. He can't come after Slaten now and Mom is talking about divorcing him. I think Aunt Beverly is an evil genius. She's a horrible woman, but she likes the idea of the merger so she sent Mom pictures of Dad kicking a puppy or something. You know Mom. She hates humans but loves those mean corgis of hers. I swear she trains them to pee on my shoes. So now he's going to be fighting that battle and we'll have time to merge the companies and live happily ever after."

A little chaos could definitely be his friend.

"I managed to work some magic for you here." Amy slipped her hand into his.

"Seriously? Did the new bed come in?" Because damn he missed his California king.

"It's currently taking up our entire bedroom," she groused with the sweetest frown. "We're moving and soon. No, I was talking about something else. Apparently when you trick a sub at Sanctum the only way to get back in is to marry her and make her very happy. Wade is going to put us through a few tests and then we'll be able to play."

He breathed a sigh of relief. He was fairly certain Wade would find a reason to send him to Butt Plugging 101 where he had to take a plug, but he would do anything to get back to the place where they fell in love. "I'm so glad, pet. You have no idea how happy that makes me."

"And I've already got the plot for your book," Bridget said with a grin.

Will groaned. "She's turned you into triplets, Flynn. Count yourself lucky. There were like five of me. I have no idea how I would handle five of me."

Bridget's wink told him she knew. "It's just a fantasy, babe. You're more man than I can handle."

"I'm going to get this one home. I'm sure he's tired." Amy held her sister's hand. "Love you."

Bridget squeezed it. "You too, sis."

She turned and walked to him. "Ready?"

With her by his side, he was ready for anything.

Author's Note

I'm often asked by generous readers how they can help get the word out about a book they enjoyed. There are so many ways to help an author you like. Leave a review. If your e-reader allows you to lend a book to a friend, please share it. Go to Goodreads and connect with others. Recommend the books you love because stories are meant to be shared. Thank you so much for reading this book and for supporting all the authors you love!

Dominance Never Dies
Masters and Mercenaries 11
By Lexi Blake

A loss he can't forget

Since losing his twin brother, Theo, in the line of duty, Case Taggart has felt dead inside. The former Navy SEAL has dedicated himself to his family and their business but he can't help but feel stuck as he watches everyone else move on with their lives. Only meeting the beautiful Mia brings Case out of his misery, until he discovered she was just a reporter looking for a story. Betrayed, he turned his back on her and never looked back.

An attraction she can't deny

Mia Danvers can't get Case Taggart out of her head. Though they hadn't been lovers, she'd felt more for him than for any man she'd ever met. Growing up in the shadow of her over-protective, older brothers, she felt free when she was with Case and she longs to feel that way again. She knows that if she can find any trace of Theo Taggart, Case will be forced to let her back into his life. Months of searching have finally paid off and she knows this is her second chance.

A desperate search

Case and Mia follow the clues they hope will lead them to Theo and the villainous Hope McDonald, but the search becomes increasingly dangerous. From Dallas to South America and beyond, dark forces work against them and threaten their lives. With each step forward, Case and Mia are pulled closer together and forced to confront their mutual attraction. But when the truth about Theo is revealed, Case may have to make a choice between his brother and the only woman he's ever loved.

* * * *

Case forced himself to stop. He pulled away from the drugging kisses she was giving him. He couldn't go down that path. If he was going to take her, it would be on his terms and that meant he wasn't going to play the idiot. He wasn't going to ask for more than she could give him. He wasn't going to pretend this was some grand love. She wasn't Charlotte and he wasn't Ian. They didn't get that forever thing.

But they could have this.

"What's wrong?" She looked up at him and then started to pull away.

He wasn't going to let that happen. He turned her around so his front nestled her back. "Nothing's wrong. I want to feel you. Do you have any idea how long I've waited to touch you, Mia? How often I've thought about this?" His hands were on her waist and he brought them up slowly. "I want to memorize every inch of your skin, and do you know how I'm going to do it?"

She leaned back into him. "You're going to touch me."

He loved how breathless she was. No other woman ever responded as honestly to him as she did. He could trust her body even if he didn't trust the rest of her. Oh, she wouldn't mean to hurt him. He actually believed that, but she would choose her world. She would choose her family over him. He could keep her for a little while.

"What am I going to touch you with, princess?" He moved slowly, letting his hands find the warm skin under her shirt.

"Your hands." Her head fell back against his chest. Without heels on she didn't quite reach his shoulders. "I want your hands everywhere, Case. They feel so good."

"I will touch you everywhere, but that's not all I'll do." He was right under her breasts. This was one of the things D/s had taught him. Sex required discipline. Patience. Control. He wanted to shove her on that bed and force his dick inside her, but that wouldn't make it good for her. This methodical arousal of every inch of her body would make her ready for him, would make her scream for him.

Might make her stay with him for a while.

He flattened one palm on the curve of her belly, the other touching the band of her bra. There was zero reason to hide how hard he was. He let his cock rub against her backside. "I'm going to put my hands on you. I'll touch your breasts and cup that hot ass of yours and I will let my fingers explore how hot and wet your pussy gets for me."

"You're killing me, Case." She squirmed a little, as though trying to get him to move.

He held her tight, his mouth against her ear. "Don't. We haven't talked about punishments so I'm not going to stop and spank that sweet ass, but now you've been warned. This is my time. It's my time to explore your body and get you hot. I'll give you time later, but for now you'll let me enjoy how you feel under my hands."

"D/s sucks," she said with a shaky laugh.

He ran the tip of his tongue along her ear, enjoying the way she shivered. "No it doesn't. It makes us take things slow and really get to know each other's bodies and responses. It makes thoughtful lovers. I want to be your lover, Mia. Do you understand what I mean by that? I don't want to be your boyfriend. I want to be your Dom. It's different. A boyfriend can take you or leave you. A Dom is responsible for you. It means something deeper to me."

"I've had boyfriends and not one of them made me feel the way you do," she admitted. "Please don't stop. I've waited so long for this."

He could smell her shampoo and the soap she used. He leaned down and ran his nose along the graceful column of her throat. "When I'm done touching you, I'm going to taste you." He ran his tongue from her collarbone back up to her ear. "I'm going to lick you and we'll see how you like a little bite."

He nipped at her ear, just a little sharp bite that made her jump in his arms. She groaned, but it wasn't one that told him she was in pain.

"I think I like it, Case," she replied, her breath shaky. "The training course alone taught me that."

He growled. "I don't like the thought of someone else training you."

Her body shook with her husky chuckle. "Javier and I were just friends. Promise. I liked the flogger he owned more than him. I liked the sting. I thought I could maybe survive a thud, but I got so hot when he hit me with the stinger. I wasn't thinking about him though. I always thought of you. It was never him holding that son of a bitch and making me beg for more."

Fuck, she could talk dirty, too, and that did something for him. "I didn't bring a flogger with me. I should have been more optimistic, but I think you'll find I can still take care of you. I'll find all kinds of things to torture you with, princess. But first I'm going to touch everything that just became mine."

Luscious

Masters and Mercenaries: Topped, Book 1
By Lexi Blake

A man who lost his future…

Macon Miles knows what it means to make sacrifices for his country. Married to his high school sweetheart, he once had a promising future in the military and everything seemed complete. All that changed when a routine patrol in Afghanistan turned into a nightmare. When the dust settled, Macon had lost his career, his wife, and his leg. Lost and alone, his only comfort comes from his newfound love of cooking. When his estranged brother, Adam, offers him a new home and a chance to work at a friend's restaurant in Dallas, it's an offer he can't refuse.

A woman searching for the past…

Allyson Jones made her foster mother a deathbed promise. She would find out what really happened to Ronnie in Afghanistan. Ally doesn't believe the Army's reports about her foster brother's death, and she knows only one man can tell her what really happened—Macon Miles. Following him to Dallas, she gets a job working alongside him at Top, Sean Taggart's decadent new restaurant. She is sure Macon is hiding something about Ronnie's death, and she'll do whatever it takes to unravel the mystery.

When circumstances force Macon and Ally together, their chemistry is hotter than any dish at Top. But when Ally's deception is exposed and the truth about Ronnie's death is revealed, will they be able to reclaim the love they've lost?

* * * *

"Are you living in your car?" Macon asked.

 She waved that off with a laugh. "Oh, that. Yes. I can't afford a place close to work yet. I'll find something in a couple of weeks."

He didn't understand her. She was acting like homelessness was a nothing problem she would deal with later. "It's dangerous."

"No more so than anywhere else. I wasn't exactly safe here at work earlier. At least I can lock the doors. And the horn makes a really good deterrent. Not to mention my LifeHammer. Sounds silly. It's really supposed to be for breaking a window if your car goes under-water. Not surprisingly, it also works on car thieves and pushy drug dealers."

She was going to give him a heart attack. "You took a hammer to a guy trying to jack your car?"

One shoulder shrugged and she went back to sweeping. "Yeah. After I brought that sucker down on his hand, he decided to try again elsewhere. And the drug dealer was actually kind of nice. I mean in the beginning. He was just getting started and his sales pitch needed work. Then he tried to rob me and he met my life hammer, too."

He opened his mouth but nothing came out. What was he supposed to say to that?

She kept on. "I would have called the cops, but I don't exactly have a cell. It's sweet of you to tell me how to protect myself. Oddly, most guys who intend to harm me don't give me lectures on protecting myself."

The rain was starting to come down hard, beating against the rooftop. He finally managed to find some proper words. "You can't stay in your car."

"Sure I can."

His first instinct was to tell her what she was going to do, but he had to wonder if she would come after him with that hammer. The woman in front of him was a far cry from the one who hadn't screamed out when Timothy cornered her. He was smart enough to understand. She was comfortable with him. She could joke because she didn't believe he would hurt her. If he applied some pressure, intimidated her, he would likely get her to do what he wanted. And that would make him one more asshole who used her. "It makes me nervous. Especially on a night like this. Maybe you could stay in Sean's office tonight?"

He would sleep on the floor. He hadn't been joking. He'd slept in much worse places. Hell, no one was shooting at him. He called it a win.

"You think you should drive home in this mess?" She peeked

out through the blinds.

"I don't have a car. I take the train. Station's right down the street." He would rather stay with her, but now that he thought about it, she might be uncomfortable with that. If he was leaving, he would have to be fast though. DART didn't run all night. He could call Adam, but he felt like an idiot calling his big brother to pick him up from work. He was thirty years old. He'd been driving since he was sixteen.

He couldn't work the gas pedal anymore and getting a vehicle fitted for him would cost more money than he had.

She perked up. "I have a car. I can totally give you a ride. And the good news is if we find ourselves in high water, I can also smash through the windshield."

"You are entirely too invested in that hammer."

She chuckled. "Maybe. I'm really okay, Miles. Despite the idiocy of this afternoon, I've been taking care of myself for a long time. It's not the first time I've been on my own. Hell, I have a car. It's practically the Ritz compared to some of the places I've slept."

"You've been homeless before?" He'd had a rough childhood. Not financially. He'd had all the money he needed, but he'd been raised in military academies, and they weren't the best at giving a child affection. Talking to Kai for all these weeks had taught him that affection was something he needed. But he couldn't imagine being a homeless kid.

"Sure. I was once given a blue ribbon by this cop in my hometown. He said I was the best runaway he'd ever seen. I might have said I couldn't be too good since he kept catching me, but he told me he liked to reward persistence."

"What were you running away from?" He asked the question, but had an idea. She could go up against drug dealers and car thieves, but she turned into a mouse around an authority figure trying to take advantage of her.

"My dad was kind of a jerk." She finished sweeping up and turned to him. "Did I say thank you for saving me today? I don't usually play the damsel in distress but you were a damn fine knight."

"There's no shining armor here, sweetheart." He'd given that up long ago. Actually, when he really thought about it, he'd never been the type.

"Let's see. You served your country honorably, you help out your boss, save waitresses from nasty assholes. You're looking pretty shiny to me, Miles."

She set the broom aside and something shifted in the room. He could see it in the way she relaxed as she moved toward him.

What was she doing? The air suddenly seemed more sultry than before. "I'm no hero. I went in the Army because it was expected of me."

"That's what a hero usually says. Why were you really looking for me, Miles?" She stepped up, leaving very little space between them.

"I told you."

"Yes, you wanted to find out about my living situation. Do you treat all the waitresses like this?"

"No." He tended to leave them alone. They were attractive women, but he didn't have anything to offer a girlfriend. He could barely take care of himself. He knew he should stay away from her, too, but she moved him in a way he hadn't felt before.

"So why me?"

"I like you." Yep he sounded like a junior high kid.

"I like you, too. I didn't think I would, but I can't deny it." She went up on her toes and her hands were suddenly flat against his chest. "This is a mistake. It's a horrible mistake, and I hope you're smart enough to stop me."

She was straining, lifting herself up as tall as she could go.

"I'm not that smart, sweetheart." He lowered his head and let his lips touch hers.

His whole body went on alert. His cock tightened immediately and his body felt like it locked around hers. All he could see or smell or taste was Ally. She became the freaking center of his universe and all he'd done was brush his lips against hers.

He was in too deep, but there was no way he was backing away now.

About Lexi Blake

New York Times bestselling author Lexi Blake lives in North Texas with her husband and three kids. Since starting her publishing journey in 2010, she's sold over three million copies of her books. She began writing at a young age, concentrating on plays and journalism. It wasn't until she started writing romance that she found success. She likes to find humor in the strangest places and believes in happy endings.

Connect with Lexi online:

Facebook: Lexi Blake
Website: www.LexiBlake.net
Instagram: AuthorLexiBlake

Sign up for Lexi's free newsletter.

www.ingramcontent.com/pod-product-compliance
Lightning Source LLC
Chambersburg PA
CBHW050845180626
46814CB00007B/2628